C. J. C

SUNFALL

Mandarin

A Mandarin Paperback

SUNFALL

First published in Great Britain
by Futura Publications
This edition published 1990
Reprinted 1990
by Mandarin Paperbacks
Michelin House, 81 Fulham Road, London SW3 6RB

Mandarin is an imprint of the Octopus Publishing Group

Copyright © 1981 by C. J. Cherryh;
by arrangement with Daw Books Inc, New York

A CIP catalogue record for this book
is available from the British Library
ISBN 0 7493 0356 5

Printed in Great Britain
by Cox & Wyman Ltd, Reading

Contents

Prologue

On the whole land surface of the Earth and on much of the seas, humankind had lived and died. In the world's youth the species had drawn together in the basins of its great rivers, the Nile, the Euphrates, the Indus; had come together in valleys to till the land; hunted the rich forests and teeming plains; herded; fished; wandered and built. In the river lands, villages grew from families; irrigated; grew; joined. Systems grew up for efficiency; and systems wanted written records; villages became towns; and towns swallowed villages and became cities.

Cities swallowed cities and became nations; nations combined into empires; conquerors were followed by law-givers who regulated the growth into new systems; systems functioned until grandsons proved less able to rule and the systems failed: again to chaos and the rise of new conquerors; endless pattern. There was no place where foot had not trod; or armies fought; and lovers sighed; and human dust settled, all unnoticed.

It was simply old, this world; had scattered its seed like a flower yielding to the winds. They had gone to the stars and gained . . . new worlds. Those who visited Earth in its great age had their own reasons . . . but those born here remained for that most ancient of reasons: it was home.

There were the cities, microcosms of human polity, great entities with much the character of individuals, which bound their residents by habit and by love and by the invisible threads that bound the first of the species to stay together, because outside the warmth of the firelit circle there was dark, and the unknown watched with wolfen eyes.

In all of human experience there was no word which encompassed this urge in all its aspects: it might have been love, but it was too often hate; it might have been community, but there was too little commonality; it might have been

unity but there was much of diversity. It was in one sense remarkable that mankind had never found a word apt for it,
and in another sense not remarkable at all. There had always
been such things too vast and too human to name: like the
reason of love and the logic in climbing mountains.

It was home, that was all.

And the cities were the last flourishing of this tendency, as
they had been its beginning.

THE ONLY DEATH IN THE CITY

(Paris)

It was named the City of Lights. It had known other names in the long history of Earth, in the years before the sun turned wan and plague-ridden, before the moon hung vast and lurid in the sky, before the ships from the stars grew few and the reasons for ambition grew fewer still. It stretched as far as the eye could see . . . if one saw it from the outside, as the inhabitants never did. It was so vast that a river flowed through it, named the Sin, which in the unthinkable past had flowed through a forest of primeval beauty, and then through a countless succession of cities, through ancient ages of empires. The City grew about the Sin, and enveloped it, so that, stone-channelled, it flowed now through the halls of the City, thundering from the tenth to the fourteenth level in a free fall, and flowing meekly along the channel within the fourteenth, a grand canal which supplied the City and made it self-sufficient. The Sin came from the outside, but it was so changed and channelled that no one remembered that this was so. No one remembered the outside. No one cared. The City was sealed, and had been so for thousands of years.

There *were* windows, but they were on the uppermost levels, and they were tightly shuttered. The inhabitants feared the sun, for popular rumor held that the sun was a source of vile radiations, unhealthful, a source of plagues. There were windows, but no doors, for no one would choose to leave. No one ever had, from the day the outer walls were built. When the City must build in this age, it built downward, digging a twentieth and twenty-first level for the burial of the dead . . . for the dead of the City were transients, in stone coffins, which might always be shifted lower still when the living needed room.

9

Once, it had been a major pastime of the City, to tour the lower levels, to seek out the painted sarcophagi of ancestors, to seek the resemblances of living face to dead so common in this long self-contained city. But now those levels were full of dust, and few were interested in going there save for funerals.

Once, it had been a delight to the inhabitants of the City to search the vast libraries and halls of art for histories, for the City lived much in the past, and reveled in old glories . . . but now the libraries went unused save for the very lightest of fictions, and those were very abstract and full of drug-dream fancies.

More and more . . . the inhabitants *remembered.*

There were a few at first who were troubled with recollections and a thorough familiarity with the halls—when once it was not uncommon to spend one's time touring the vast expanse of the City, seeing new sights. These visionaries sank into ennui . . . or into fear, when the recollections grew quite vivid.

There was no need to go to the lower levels seeking ancestors. They lived . . . incarnate in the sealed halls of the City, in the persons of their descendants, souls so long immured within the megalopolis that they began to wake to former pasts, for dying, they were reborn, and remembered, eventually. So keenly did they recall that now mere infants did not cry, but lay patiently dreaming in their cradles, or, waking, stared out from haunted eyes, gazing into mothers' eyes with millennia of accumulated lives, *aware*, and waiting on adulthood, for body to overtake memory.

Children played . . . various games, wrought of former lives.

The people lived in a curious mixture of caution and recklessness: caution, for they surrounded themselves with the present, knowing the danger of entanglements; recklessness, for past ceased to fascinate them as an unknown and nothing had permanent meaning. There was only pleasure, and the future, which held the certainty of more lives, which would remember the ones they presently lived. For a very long time, death was absent from the halls of the City of Lights.

Until one was born to them.

Only rarely there were those born new, new souls which had not made previous journeys within the City, babes which cried, children who grew up conscious of their affliction, true children among the reborn.

Such was Alain.

He was born in one of the greatest of families—those families of associations dictated more by previous lives than by blood, for while it was true that reincarnation tended to follow lines of descendancy, this was not always the case; and sometimes there were those from outside the bloodline who drifted in as children, some even in their first unsteady steps, seeking old loves, old connections. But Alain was new. He was born to the Jade Palace Family, which occupied the tenth level nearest the stairs, although he was not *of* that family or indeed of any family, and therefore grew up less civilized.

He tried. He was horribly conscious of his lack of taste, his lack of discrimination which he could not excuse as original-ity: originality was for—older—minds and memories. His be-havior was simply awkward, and he stayed much in the shadows in Jade Palace, enduring this life and thinking that his next would surely be better.

But Jade was neighbor to Onyx Palace, and it was inevi-table that these two houses mix upon occasion of anniver-saries. These times were Alain's torment when he was a child, when his naïve and real childhood was exposed to outsiders; they became torment of a different kind in his fourteenth year, when suddenly his newly maturing discrimination settled upon a certain face, a certain pale loveliness in the Onyx House.

"Only to be expected," his mother sighed. He had embar-rassed her many times, and diffidently came to her now with this confession . . . that he had seen in this Onyx princess what others saw within their own houses; an acuteness of longing possessed him which others claimed only for old recognitions and old lovers of former lives. He was new, and it was for the first time. "Her name," his mother asked.

"Ermine," he whispered, his eyes downcast upon the pat-terns of the carpets, which his aunt had loomed herself in a long-past life. "Her name is Ermine."

"Boy," his mother said, "you are a droplet in the canal of *her* lives. Forget her."

It was genuine pity he heard in his mother's voice, and this was very rare. *You entertain me,* was the kindest thing she had yet said to him, high compliment, implying he might yet attain to novelty. Now her kind advice brought tears to his eyes, but he shook his head, looked up into her eyes, which he did seldom: they were very old and very wise and he sensed them forever comparing him to memories ages past.

"Does anyone," he asked, "ever forget?"

"Boy, I give you good advice. Of course I can't stop you. You'll be born a thousand times and so will she, and you'll never make up for your youth. But such longings come out again if they're not checked, in this life or the next, and they make misery. Sleep with many; make good friends, who may be born in your next life; no knowing whether you'll be man or woman or if they'll be what they are. Make many friends, that's my advice to you, so that whether some are born ahead of you and some behind, whether sexes are what they are . . . there'll be *some* who'll be glad to see you among them. That's how one makes a place for one's self. I did it ages ago before I began to remember my lives. But I've every confidence you'll remember yours at once; that's the way things are, now. And when you've a chance to choose intelligently as you do in these days, why, lad, be very glad for good advice. Don't set your affections strongly in your very first life. Make no enemies either. Think of your uncle Legran and Pertito, who kill each other in every life they live, whatever they are. Never set strong patterns. Be wise. A pattern set so early could make all your lives tragedy."

"I love her," he said with all the hopeless fervor of his fourteen unprefaced years.

"Oh my dear," his mother said, and sadly shook her head. She was about to tell him one of her lives, he knew, and he looked again at the carpet, doomed to endure it.

He did not see Onyx Ermine again that year, not the next nor the two succeeding: his mother maneuvered the matter very delicately and he was thwarted. But in his eighteenth year the quarrel Pertito had with uncle Legran broke into feud, and his mother died, stabbed in the midst of the argument.

Complications, she had warned him. He stood looking at her coffin the day of the funeral and fretted bitterly for the loss of her who had been his best and friendliest advisor, fretted also for her sake, that she had been woven into a pattern she had warned him to avoid. Pertito and Legran were both there, looking hate at one another. "You've involved Claudette," Pertito had shouted at Legran while she lay dying on the carpet between them; and the feud was more bitter between the two than it had ever been, for they had both loved

Claudette, his mother. It would not be long, he thought with
the limits of his experience in such matters, before Pertito
and Legran would follow her. He was wise and did not hate
them, wrenched himself away from the small gathering of
family and wider collection of curious outside Jade Palace,
for he had other things to do with his lives, and he thought
that his mother would much applaud his good sense.

But while he was walking away from the gathering he saw
Ermine standing there among her kin of Onyx.

And if she had been beautiful when they were both fourteen, she was more so now. He stood and stared at her, a
vision of white silk and pearls from the Sin, of pale hair and
pink flushed skin. It was Ermine who drew him back to his
mother's funeral . . . Claudette, he must think of his mother
now, by her true name, for she had stopped being his mother,
and might at this moment be born far across the City, to begin her journey back to them. This mourning was only cere-
mony, a farewell of sorts, excuse for a party. It grew, as they
walked the stairs past the thundering waters of the Sin, as
more and more curious attached themselves and asked who
had died, and how, and the tale was told and retold at other
levels. But it was the kin who really knew her who did the
telling; in his own low estate he kept silent and soon grew
disaffected from all the empty show . . . his eyes were only
for Ermine.

He moved to her side as they walked constantly down the
long stairs which wrapped the chute of the Sin. "Might we
meet after?" he asked, not looking at her, for shyness was the
rule of his life.

He felt her look at him; at least he perceived a movement,
a certain silence, and the heat crept to his face. "I think we
might," she said, and his heart pounded in his breast.

Never set strong patterns, Claudette had warned him; and
before her body was entombed her voice seemed far away,
and her advice less wise than it had seemed. After all, *she*
had passed that way, and he was about to live life on his
own.

I shall be wise, he promised her ghost. Claudette would be
a child of his generation, surely . . . perhaps . . . the
thought stunned him, perhaps his own with Ermine's. She
would be very welcome if she were. He would tell her so
many things that he would have learned by then. It would be
one of those rare, forever marriages, himself with Ermine;

Ermine would love him . . . such a drawing could not be one-sided. The feeling soaring in him was the whole world and it was unreasonable to him that Ermine could go unmoved.

He was four years wiser than he had been, and filled with all the history he had been able to consume by reading and listening.

Pertito and Legran argued loudly near him. He paid them no heed. They reached the level of the tombs, far below the course of the Sin, and with great solemnity—all of them loved pomp when there was excuse for it—conveyed Claudette to her tomb. The populace was delighted when Pertito accused Legran of the murder; was elated when the whole funeral degenerated into a brawl, and the Pertito/Legran quarrel embroiled others. It found grand climax when knives were drawn, and uncle Legran and Pertito vowed suicide to expiate the wrong done Claudette. This was a grand new turn to the centuries-old drama, and the crowd gasped and applauded, profoundly delighted by a variation in a vendetta more than thirty centuries old. The two walked ahead of the returning crowd, and from the tenth level, leaped into the chute of the Sin, to the thunderous applause of much of the City. Everyone was cheerful, anticipating a change in the drama in their next lives. Novelty—it was so rarely achieved, and so to be savored. The souls of Pertito and Legran would be welcomed wherever they incarnated, and there would be an orgy to commemorate the day's grand events, in the fond hope of hastening the return of the three most delightsome participants in the cycles of the City.

And Jade Alain fairly skipped up the long, long stairs above the thundering flood of the Sin, to change his garments for festal clothes, his very best, and to attend on Onyx Ermine.

He decked himself in sable and the green and white stones of his name, and with a smile on his face and a lightness in his step he walked to the doors of Onyx Palace.

There were no locks, of course, nor guards. The criminals of the City were centuries adept and not so crude. He walked in quite freely as he had come in company to the great anniversaries of the houses, asked of an Onyx child where might be the princess Ermine. The wise-eyed child looked him up and down and solemnly led him through the maze of corridors, into a white and yellow hall, where Ermine sat in a cluster of young friends.

"Why, it's the Jade youth," she said delightedly.

"It's Jade Alain," another yawned. "He's very new."

"Go away," Ermine bade them all. They departed in no great haste. The bored one paused to look Alain up and down, but Alain avoided the eyes . . . looked up only when he was alone with Ermine.

"Come here," she said. He came and knelt and pressed her hand.

"I've come," he said, "to pay you court, Onyx Ermine."

"To sleep with me?"

"To pay you court," he said. "To marry you."

She gave a little laugh. "I'm not wont to marry. I have very seldom married."

"I love you," he said. "I've loved you for four years."

"Only that?" Her laugh was sweet. He looked up into her eyes and wished that he had not, for the age that was there. "Four years," she mocked him. "But how old are you, Jade Alain?"

"It's," he said in a faint voice, "my first life. And I've never loved anyone but you."

"Charming," she said, and leaned and kissed him on the lips, took both his hands and drew them to her heart. "And shall we be lovers this afternoon?"

He accepted. It was a delirium, a dream half true. She brought him through halls of white and yellow stone and into a room with a bed of saffron satin. They made love there all the afternoon, though he was naïve and she sometimes laughed at his innocence; though sometimes he would look by mistake into her eyes and see all the ages of the City looking back at him. And at last they slept; and at last they woke.

"Come back again," she said, "when you're reborn. We shall find pleasure in it."

"Ermine," he cried. "Ermine!"

But she left the bed and shrugged into her gown, called attendants and lingered there among the maids, laughter in her aged eyes. "In Onyx Palace, newborn lover, the likes of you are servants . . . like these, even after several lifetimes. What decadences Jade tolerates to bring one up a prince! You have diverted me, put a crown on a memorable day. Now begone. I sense myself about to be bored."

He was stunned. He sat a good long moment after she had

left in the company of her maids, heart-wounded and with heat flaming in his face. But then, the reborn were accustomed to speak to him and to each other with the utmost arrogance. He thought it a testing, as his mother had tested him, as Pertito and Legran had called him hopelessly young, but not without affection . . . He thought, sitting there, and thought, when he had dressed to leave . . . and concluded that he had not utterly failed to amuse. It was novelty he lacked.

He might achieve this by some flamboyance, a fourth Jade death . . . hastening into that next life . . . but he would miss Onyx Ermine by the years that she would continue to live, and he would suffer through lifetimes before they were matched in age again.

He despaired. He dressed again and walked out to seek her in the halls, found her at last in the company of Onyx friends, and the room echoing with laughter.

At him.

It died for a moment when she saw him standing there. She held out her hand to him with displeasure in eyes, and he came to her, stood among them.

There was a soft titter from those around her.

"You should have sent him to me," a woman older than the others whispered, and there was general laughter.

"For you there *is* no novelty," Ermine laughed. She lolled carelessly upon her chair and looked up at Alain. "Do go now, before you become still more distressed. Shall I introduce you to my last husband?" She stroked the arm of the young woman nearest her. "She was. But that was very long ago. And already you are dangerously predictable. I fear I shall be bored."

"Oh, how can we be?" the woman who had been her husband laughed. "We shall be entertained at Jade's expense for years. He's very determined. Just look at him. This is the sort of fellow who can make a pattern, isn't he? Dear Ermine, he'll plague us all before he's done, create some nasty scandal and we shall all be like Legran and Pertito and poor Claudette . . . or whatever their names will be. We shall be sitting in this room cycle after cycle fending away this impertinent fellow."

"How distressing," someone yawned.

The laughter rippled round again, and Ermine rose from her chair, took his burning face in her two hands and smiled at him. "I cannot even remember being the creature you are. There is no hope for you. Don't you know that I'm one of the oldest in Onyx? You've had your education. Begone."

"Four years," someone laughed. "She won't look at me after thirty lifetimes."

"Good-bye," she said.

"What might I do," he asked quietly, "to convince you of novelty and persuade you, in this life or the next?"

Then she did laugh, and thought a moment. "Die the death for love of me. No one has done that."

"And will you marry me before that? It's certain there's no bargain after."

There was a shocked murmur among her friends, and the flush drained from the cheeks of Onyx Ermine.

"He's quite mad," someone said.

"Oynx offered a wager," he said. "Jade would never say what it doesn't mean. Shall I tell this in Jade, and amuse my elders with the tale?"

"I shall give you four years," she said, "since you reckon that a very long time."

"You will marry me."

"You will die the death after that fourth year, and I shall not be bothered with you in the next life."

"No," he said. "You will not be bothered."

There was no more laughter. He had achieved novelty. The older woman clapped her hands solemnly, and the others joined the applause. Ermine inclined her head to them, and to him; he bowed to all of them in turn.

"Arrange it," she said.

It was a grand wedding, the more so because weddings were rare, on the banks of the Sin where alone in the City there was room enough to contain the crowd. Alain wore black with white stones; Ermine wore white with yellow gold. There was dancing and feasting and the dark waters of the Sin glistened with the lights of lanterns and sparkling fires, with jewel-lights and the glowing colors of the various palaces of the City.

And afterward there was long, slow lovemaking, while the celebrants outside the doors of Jade Palace drank themselves giddy and feted a thing no one had ever seen, so bizarre a bargain, with all honor to the pair which had contrived it.

In days following the wedding all the City filed into Jade

to pay courtesy, and to see the wedded couple . . . to applaud politely the innovation of the youngest and most tragic prince of the City. It was the more poignant because it was real tragedy. It eclipsed that of the Grand Cyclics. It was one of the marks of the age, an event unduplicatable, and no one wished to miss it.

Even the Death came, almost the last of the visitors, and that was an event which crowned all the outré affair, an arrival which struck dumb those who were in line to pay their respects and rewarded those who happened to be there that day with the most bizarre and terrible vision of all.

She had come far, up all the many turnings of the stairs from the nether depths of the City, where she kept her solitary lair near the tombs. She came robed and veiled in black, a spot of darkness in the line. At first no one realized the nature of this guest, but all at once the oldest did, and whispered to the others.

Onyx Ermine knew, being among the oldest, and rose from her throne in sudden horror. Alain stood and held Ermine's hand, with a sinking in his heart.

Their guest came closer, swathed in her robes . . . she, rumor held it, had a right to Jade, who had been born here—not born at all, others said, but engendered of all the deaths the City never died. She drank souls and lives. She had prowled among them in the ancient past like a beast, taking the unwilling, appearing where she would in the shadows. But at last she established herself by the tombs below, for she found some who sought her, those miserable in their incarnations, those whose every life had become intolerable pain. She was the only death in the City from which there was no rebirth.

She was the one by whom the irreverent swore, lacking other terrors.

"Go away," the eldest of Jade said to her.

"But I have come to the wedding," the Death said. It was a woman's voice beneath the veils. "Am I not party to this? I was not consulted, but shall I not agree?"

"We have heard," said Onyx Ermine, who was of too many lifetimes to be set back for long, "we have heard that you are not selective."

"Ah," said the Death. "Not lately indeed; so few have come to me. But shall I not seal the bargain?"

There was silence, dread silence. And with a soft whisper-

ing of her robes the Death walked forward, held out her
hands to Jade Alain, leaned forward for a kiss.

He bent, shut his eyes, for the veil was gauze, and he had
no wish to see. It was hard enough to bear the eyes of the
many-lived; he had no wish at all to gaze into hers, to see
what rumor whispered he should find there, all the souls she
had ever drunk. Her lips were warm through the gauze,
touched lightly, and her hands on his were delicate and kind.

She walked away then. He felt Ermine's hand take his,
cold and sweating. He settled again into the presence hall
throne and Ermine took her seat beside him. There was awe
on faces around them, but no applause.

"She has come out again," someone whispered. "And she
hasn't done that in ages. But I remember the old days. She
may hunt again. She's *awake,* and interested."

"It's Onyx's doing," another voice whispered. And in that
coldness the last of the wedding guests drifted out.

The doors of Jade Palace closed. "Bar them," the eldest
said. It was for the first time in centuries.

And Ermine's hand lay very cold in Alain's.

"Madam," he said, "are you satisfied?"

She gave no answer, nor spoke of it after.

There were seasons in the City. They were marked in anniversaries of the Palaces, in exquisite entertainments, in
births and deaths.

The return of Claudette was one such event, when a year-
old child with wise blue eyes announced his former name,
and old friends came to toast the occasion.

The return of Legran and Pertito was another, for they
were twin girls in Onyx, and this complication titillated the
whole City with speculations which would take years to
prove.

The presence of Jade Alain at each of these events was remarked with a poignancy which satisfied everyone with sensi-
tivity, in the remarkable realization that Onyx Ermine, who
hid in disgrace, would inevitably return to them, and this
most exquisite of youths would not.

One of the greatest Cycles and one of the briefest lives existed in intimate connection. It promised change.

And as for the Death, she had no need to hunt, for the
lesser souls, seeking to imitate fashion in this drama, flocked
to her lair in unusual number . . . some curious and some

self-destructive, seeking their one great moment of passion
and notoriety, when a thousand thousand years had failed to
give them fame.

They failed of it, of course, for such demises were only following a fashion, not setting one; and they lacked inven-
tiveness in their endings as in their lives.

It was for the fourth year the City waited.

And in its beginning:

"It is three-fourths gone," Onyx Ermine said. She had
grown paler still in her shamed confinement within Jade
Palace. In days before this anniversary of their wedding she
had received old friends from Onyx, the first time in their
wedded life she had received callers. He had remarked then a
change in her lovemaking, that what had been pleasantly in-
different acquired . . . passion. It was perhaps the rise in ·her
spirits. There were other possibilities, involving a former
lover. He was twenty-two and saw things more clearly than
once he had.

"You will be losing something," he reminded her coldly,
"beyond recall and without repetition. That should enliven
your long life."

"Ah," she said, "don't speak of it. I repent the bargain. I
don't want this horrid thing, I don't; I don't want you to die."

"It's late for that," he said.

"I love you."

That surprised him, brought a frown to his brow and almost a warmth to his heart, but he could muster only
sadness. "You don't," he said. "You love the novelty I've
brought. You have never loved a living being, not in all your
lifetimes. You never could have loved. That is the nature of
Onyx."

"No. You don't know. Please. Jade depresses me. Please
let's go and spend the year in Onyx, among my friends. I
must recover them, build back my old associations. I shall be
all alone otherwise. If you care anything at all for my happiness, let's go home to Onyx."

"If you wish," he said, for it was the first time that she had
shown him her heart, and he imagined that it might be very
fearsome for one so long incarnate in one place to spend too
much time apart from it. His own attachments were ephem-
eral. "Will it make you content?"

"I shall be very grateful," she said, and put her arms about
his neck and kissed him tenderly.

They went that day, and Onyx received them, a restrained but festive occasion as befitted Ermine's public disfavor . . . but she fairly glowed with life, as if all the shadows she had dreaded in Jade were gone. "Let us make love," she said, "oh now!" And they lay all afternoon in the saffron bed, a slow and pleasant time.

"You're happy," he said to her. "You're finally happy."

"I love you," she whispered in his ear as they dressed for dinner, she in her white and pearls and he in his black and his green jade. "Oh let us stay here and not think of other things."

"Or of year's end?" he asked, finding that thought incredibly difficult, this day, to bear.

"Hush," she said, and gave him white wine to drink.

They drank together from opposite sides of one goblet, sat down on the bed and mingled wine and kisses. He felt strangely numb, lay back, with the first intimation of betrayal. He watched her cross the room, open the door. A tear slipped from his eye, but it was anger as much as pain.

"Take him away," Onyx Ermine whispered to her friends. "Oh take him quickly and end this. *She* will not care if he comes early."

"The risk we run . . ."

"Would you have her come *here?* For three years I have lived in misery, seeing *her* in every shadow. I can't bear it longer. I can't bear touching what I'm going to lose. Take him there. Now."

He tried to speak. He could not. They wrapped him in the sheets and satin cover and carried him, a short distance at first, and then to the stairs, by many stages. He heard finally the thunder of the falls of the Sin, and the echoes of the lower levels . . . heard the murmur of spectators near him at times, and knew that none but Jade might have interfered. They were all merely spectators. That was all they wished to be, to avoid complications.

Even, perhaps, Jade itself . . . observed.

They laid him down at last in a place where feet scuffed dryly on dust, and fled, and left silence and dark. He lay long still, until a tingling in his fingers turned to pain, which traveled all his limbs and left him able again to move. He stirred, and staggered to his feet, cold in a bitter wind, chilled by the lonely dark. From before him came the dim light of lamps, and a shadow sat between them.

"You are betrayed," the Death said.

He wrapped his arms about him against the chill and stared at her.

"She doesn't love you," said the Death. "Don't you know that?"

"I knew," he said. "But then, no one ever did. They've forgotten how."

The Death lifted her hands to the veils and let them fall. She was beautiful, pale of skin, with ebon hair and a blood-red stain of rubies at her brow. She held out hands to him, rising. And when she came to him he did not look away. "Some change their minds," she said. "Even those who come of their own will."

The eyes were strange, constantly shifting in subtle tones . . . the fires, perhaps, or all the souls she had drunk, all the torment. "I bring peace," she said. "If I did not exist, there would be no way out. And they would all go mad. I am their choice. I am possibility. I am change in the cycles."

He gazed into the flickerings, the all-too-tenanted eyes. "How is it done?" he asked, fearing to know.

She embraced him, and laid her head at his shoulder. He flinched from a tiny sharp pain at his throat, quickly done. A chill grew in his limbs, a slight giddiness like love.

"Go back," she said releasing him. "Run away until your time."

He stumbled back, found the door, realized belatedly her words.

"Go," she said. "I'll come for you . . . in my agreed time. I at least keep my word, Jade Alain."

And when he would have gone. . . .

"Jade Alain," she said. "I know you have moved to Onyx. I know most things in the City. Tell your wife . . . I keep my promises."

"She fears you."

"She is nothing," the Death said. "Do you fear me?"

He considered. The question found him numb. And for all his numbness he walked back to her, faced the dreadful eyes. He tested his courage by it. He tested it further, took the Death's face between his hands and returned the kiss she had given three years before.

"Ah," she said. "That was kind."

"You are gentle," he said. "I shall not mind."

"Sad Jade prince. Go. Go away just now."

He turned away, walked out the grim doorway into the light, walked up the stairs, a long, long walk, in which there were few passersby, for it was what passed for night in the City now, and of that he was very glad, because of the shame which Onyx had dealt him and the anger he felt. Those who did see him stared, and muttered behind their hands and shrank away. So did those at the doors of Onyx, who blanched and began to bar his way.

But the doors opened, and Ermine's several friends stood with knives.

"Go away," they said.

"That was not the bargain," he replied.

"Your wife is the bargain," the oldest woman said. "Take Ermine back to Jade. Don't involve us."

"*No,*" Ermine wailed from the hall beyond; but they brought her to him, and he took her by the hand and dragged her along to his own doors. She ceased struggling. They entered within the ornate halls of Jade Palace, and under the fearful eyes of his own kin, he drew her through the maze of corridors to his own apartments, and sealed the door fast behind them.

She was there. There was no possible means that she could be . . . but there the Death stood, clothed in black, among the green draperies by the bed. Ermine flung about and cried aloud, stopped by his opposing arms.

"Go," the Death said. "I've nothing to do with you yet. Your wife and I have business."

He held Ermine still, she shivering and holding to him and burying her face against him. He shook his head. "No," he said, "I can't. I can't give her to you."

"I've been offended," the Death said. "How am I to be paid for such an offense against my dignity?"

He thought a moment. Smoothed Ermine's pale hair. "The year that I have left. What is that to me? Don't take Ermine's lives. She cares so much to save them."

"Does Ermine agree?" the Death asked.

"Yes," Ermine sobbed, refusing to look back.

He sighed, hurt at last, shook his head and put Ermine from him. The Death reached out her hand, and he came to her, embraced her, looked back as she put her black-robed arm about him. Ermine cowered in the corner, head upon her knees.

"Cousin," the Death whispered to him, for she was once of

Jade. He looked into the shifting eyes, and she touched her finger first to her lips and to his; it bled, and left the blood on his lips. "Mine," she said. "As you are."

He was. He felt cold, and hungry for life, desired it more than ever he had desired in his youth.

"I also," the Death said, "am once-born . . . and never die. Nor shall you. Nor have a name again. Nor care."

"Ermine," he whispered, to have the sight of her face again. She looked.

And screamed, and hid her face in her hands.

"When the lives grow too many," the Death said, "and you grow weary, Ermine . . . we will be waiting."

"Whenever you wish," he said to Ermine, and slipped his hand within the Death's warm hand, and went with her, the hidden ways.

Pertito shook his head sadly, poured more wine, stroked the cheek of Legran, who was his lover this cycle, and Claudette's sister. Below their vantage, beyond the balcony, a pale figure wavered on the tenth level stairs, where the Sin began its dizzying fall. "I'll wager she's on the verge again," he said. "Poor Ermine. Thousands of years and no invention left. Never more years than twenty-two. When she reaches that age . . . she's gone."

"Not this time," Legran said.

"Ah. Look. She's on the edge."

Legran stretched her neck to see, remained tranquil. "A wager?"

"Has she whispered things in your brother's ear, perhaps? Lovers' confidences?"

Legran sighed, smiled lazily, settling again. She sipped at her cup and her smoky eyes danced above the rim. A crowd was gathering to watch the impending leap.

"Do you know something?" Pertito asked.

"Ah, my tragic brother, to be in love with Ermine. Three lifetimes now he could not hold her. . . . Wager on it, my love?"

Pertito hesitated. A hundred lifetimes without variance. It was a small crowd, observing the suicide indifferently, expecting no novelty from Ermine.

"This time," Legran said, eyes dancing more, "there is a rival."

"A second lover?"

The white figure poised delicately on the topmost step of the chute. There were sighs, a polite rippling of applause.

"A very old one," Legran said. "For some months now. Ah. There she goes."

There were gasps, a dazed silence from the crowd.

Past the falls, this time, and down and down the stairs, a gleam of white and pearls.

THE HAUNTED TOWER

(London)

There were ghosts in old London, that part of London outside the walls and along the river, or at least the townsfolk outside the walls believed in them: mostly they were attributed to the fringes of the city, and the unbelievers inside the walls insisted they were manifestations of sunstruck brains, of senses deceived by the radiations of the dying star and the fogs which tended to gather near the Thames. Ghosts were certainly unfashionable for a city management which prided itself on technology, which confined most of its bulk to a well-ordered cube (geometrically perfect except for the central arch which let the Thames flow through) in which most of the inhabitants lived precisely ordered lives. London had its own spaceport, maintained offices for important offworld companies, and it thrived on trade. It pointed at other cities in its vicinity as declined and degenerate, but held itself as an excellent and enlightened government: since the Restoration and the New Mayoralty, reason reigned in London, and traditions were cultivated only so far as they added to the comfort of the city and those who ruled it. If the governed of the city believed in ghosts and other intangibles, well enough; reliance on astrology and luck and ectoplasmic utterances made it less likely that the governed would seek to analyze the governors upstairs.

There were some individuals who analyzed the nature of things, and reached certain conclusions, and who made their attempts on power.

For them the Tower existed, a second cube some distance down the river, which had very old foundations and very old traditions. The use of it was an inspiration on the part of the New Mayoralty, which studied its records and found itself a way to dispose of unwanted opinion. The city was self-contained. So was the Tower. What disappeared into the Tower only rarely reappeared . . . and the river ran between, a private, unassailable highway for the damned, so that there was no untidy publicity.

Usually the voyagers were the fallen powerful, setting out from that dire river doorway of the city of London.

On this occasion one Bettine Maunfry came down the steps toward the rusty iron boat and the waters of old Thames. She had her baggage (three big boxes) brought along by the police, and though the police were grim, they did not insult her, because of who she had been, and might be again if the unseen stars favored her.

She boarded the boat in a state of shock, sat with her hands clenched in her lap and stared at something other than the police as they loaded her baggage aboard and finally closed the door of the cabin. This part of the city was an arch above the water, a darksome tunnel agleam with lights which seemed far too few; and she swallowed and clenched her hands the more tightly as the engines began to chug their way downriver toward the daylight which showed at the end.

They came finally into the wan light of the sun, colors which spread themselves amber and orange across the dirty glass of the cabin windows. The ancient ruins of old London appeared along the banks, upthrust monoliths and pillars and ruined bits of wall which no one ever had to look at but those born outside—as she had been, but she had tried to forget that.

In not so long a time there was a smooth modern wall on the left side, which was the wall of the Tower, and the boat ground and bumped its way to the landing.

Then she must get out again, and, being frightened and unsteady, she reached out her hand for the police to help her across the narrow ramp to the shore and the open gate of that wall. They helped her and passed her on to the soldier/warders, who brought her within the gates; she stood on stones which were among the most ancient things in all of ancient London, and the steel gates, which were not at all ancient, and very solid, gaped and hissed and snicked shut with ominous authority. The chief warder, a gray-haired man, led her beyond the gatehouse and into the interior of the Tower which, to her surprise, was not a building, but a wall, girding many buildings, many of them crumbling brick and very,

very old-seeming. Guards followed with her baggage as she
walked this strange, barren courtyard among the crumbling
buildings.

"What are these stones?" she asked of the older man who
led the way, proper and militarily slim. "What are they?"

But he would not answer her, as none of them spoke to
her. They escorted her to the steps of a modern tower, which
bestraddled ancient stones and made them a part of its structure, old brick with gleaming steel. The older man showed
her through the gateway and up the steps, while the others
followed after. It was a long climb—no lift, nothing of the
sort; the lights were all shielded and the doors which they
passed were all without handles.

Third level; the chief warder motioned her through a doorway just at the top of the stairs, which led to a hall ending in
a closed door. She found the guards pushing her luggage past
her into that short corridor, and when she did not move, the
chief warder took her arm and put her through the archway,
himself staying behind. "Wait," she cried, "wait," but no one
waited and no one cared. The door shut. She wept, she beat
at the closed door with her fists, she kicked the door and
kicked it again for good measure, and finally she tried the
door at the other end of the hall, pushed the only door switch
she had, which let her into a grim, one-room apartment, part
brick and part steel, a bed which did not look comfortable,
thinly mattressed; a bathroom at least separate of the single
room, a window, a wall console: she immediately and in
panic pushed buttons there, but it was dead, quite dead.
Tears streamed down her face and she wiped them with the
back of her hand and snuffled because there was no one to
see the inelegance.

She went to the window then and looked out, saw the
courtyard and in it the guards who had brought her heading
to the gates; and the gates opening on the river and closing
again.

Fear came over her, dread that perhaps she was alone in
this place and the stones and the machines might be all there
was. She ran to the panel and punched buttons and pleaded,
and there was nothing; then she grew anxious that the apartment door might close on its own. She scurried out into the
short hallway and dragged her three cases in and sat down on
the thin mattress and cried.

Tears ran out after a time; she had done a great deal of

crying and none of it had helped, so she sat with her hands in
her lap and hoped earnestly that the screen and the phone
would come on and it would be Richard, his honor Richard
Collier the mayor, to say he had frightened her enough, and
he had.

The screen did not come on. Finally she began to snuffle
again and wiped her eyes and realized that she was staying at
least . . . at least a little time. She gathered her clothes out
of the boxes and hung them; laid out her magazines and her
books and her knitting and sewing and her jewelry and her
cosmetics and all the things she had packed. . . . At least
they had let her pack. She went into the bath and sat down
and repaired her makeup, painting on a perfectly insouciant
face, and finding in this mundane act a little comfort.

She was not the sort of person who was sent to the Tower;
she was only a girl, (though thirty) the Mayor's girl. She was
plain Bettine Maunfry. His Honor's wife knew about her and
had no resentments; it just could not be that Marge had
turned on her; she was not the first girl his Honor had had,
and not the only even at the moment. Richard was jealous,
that was all, angry when he had found out there might be
someone else, and he had power and he was using it to
frighten her. It had to be. Richard had other girls and a wife,
and there was no reason for him to be jealous. He had no
right to be jealous. But he was; and he was vindictive. And
because he was an important man, and she was no one, she
was more frightened now than she had ever been in her life.

The Tower was for dangerous criminals. But Richard had
been able to do this and get away with it, which she would
never have dreamed; it was all too cruel a joke. He had some
kind of power and the judges did what he wanted; or he
never even bothered to get a court involved.

The tears threatened again, and she sniffed and stared
without blinking at her reflected image until the tears dried.
Her face was her defense, her beauty her protection. She had
always known how to please others. She had worked all her
life at it. She had learned that this was power, from the time
she was a tiny girl, that she must let others have control of
things, but that she could play on them and get them to do
most things that she wanted. *I like people,* was the way she
put it, in a dozen variants; all of which meant that as much
as she hated technical things she liked to know all about different types of personalities; it sounded altruistic, and it also

gave her power of the kind she wanted. Most of the time she
even believed in the altruism . . . until a thing like this, until
this dreadful grim joke. This time it had not worked, and
none of this should be happening.

It would still work, if she could get face-to-face with
Richard, and not Richard the Lord Mayor. She tested a delib-
erate and winning smile in the mirror, perfect teeth, a be-
witching little twitch of a shoulder.

Downy lashes rimming blue eyes, a mouth which could
pout and tremble and reflect emotions like the breathing of
air over water, so fine, so responsive, to make a man like His
Honor feel powerful . . . that was all very well: she knew
how to do that. He *loved* her . . . after a possessive fashion;
he had never said so, but she fed his middle-aged vanity, and
that was what was hurt; that had to be it, that she had wounded him more than she had thought and he had done this, to
show her he was powerful.

But he would have to come, and see how chastened she
was and then he would feel sorry for what he had done, and
they would make up and she would be back safe in the city
again.

He would come.

She changed to her lounging gown, with a very deep neck-
line, and went back and combed her dark masses of hair
just so, just perfect with the ruby gown with the deep plunge
and the little bit of ruby glitter paler than the blood-red fab-
ric. . . . He had given that to her. He would remember that
evening when he saw her wearing it.

She waited. The silence here was deep, so, so deep. Somewhere in this great building there should be *someone* else. It
was night outside the window now, and she looked out and
could not bear to look out again, because it was only
blackness, and reminded her she was alone. She wished that
she could curtain it; she might have hung something over it,
but that would make the place look shabby, and she lived by
beauty. Survived by it. She sat down in the chair and turned
on the light and read her magazines, articles on beauty and
being desirable which now, while they had entertained her before, seemed shatteringly *important*.

Her horoscope was good; it said she should have luck in
romance. She tried to take this for hopeful. She was a Pisces.
Richard had given her this lovely charm which she wore

about her neck; the fish had real diamond eyes. He laughed at her horoscopes, but she knew they were right.

They must be this time. *My little outsider,* he called her, because like most who believed in horoscopes, she came from outside; but she had overcome her origins. She had been a beautiful child, and because her father had worked Inside, she had gotten herself educated . . . was educated, absolutely, in all those things proper for a girl, nothing serious or studious, nothing of expertise unless it was in Working With People, because she knew that it was just not smart at all for a girl to be too obviously clever . . . modesty got a girl much further . . . that and the luck of being beautiful, which let her cry prettily. Her childish tantrums had gotten swift comfort and a chuck under the chin, while her brothers got spanked, and that was the first time she had learned about *that* kind of power, which she had always had. It was luck, and that was in the stars. And her magazines told her how to be even more pleasing and pleasant and that she succeeded in what she thought she did. That it worked was self-evident: a girl like her, from the outside, and a receptionist in His Honor the Mayor's office, and kept by him in style people Outside could not imagine. . . .

Only there were bad parts to it too, and being here was one, that she had never planned for—

A door opened somewhere below. Her heart jumped. She started to spring up and then thought that she should seem casual and then that she should not, that she should seem anxious and worried, which was why Richard had sent her here. Perhaps she should cry. Perhaps it was Richard. It *must* be Richard.

She put the magazine away and fretted with her hands, for once in her life not knowing what to do with them, but even this was a pretty gesture and she knew that it was.

The door opened. It was the military warden, with dinner.

"I can't eat," she said. It seemed upon the instant that intense depression was the ploy to use. She turned her face away, but he walked in and set it on the table.

"That's your business," he said, and started to leave.

"Wait." He stopped and she turned her best pleading look on him . . . an older man and the kind who could be intensely flattered by beauty . . . flattered, if she seemed vulnerable, and she put on that air. "Please. Is there any word . . . from Richard?"

"No," he said, distressingly impervious. "Don't expect any."

"Please. Please tell him that I want to talk to him."

"If he asks."

"Please. My phone doesn't work."

"Not supposed to. It doesn't work for all prisoners. Just those with privileges. You don't have any."

"*Tell* him I want to see him. Tell him. It's his message. Won't *he* decide whether he wants to hear it?"

That got through. She saw the mouth indecisive. The man closed the door; she heard the steps going away. She clutched her hands together, finding them shaking.

And she ignored the food, got out her magazine again and tried to read, but it hardly occupied her mind. She dared not sit on the bed and prop her knees up and read; or sit down to eat; it was too informal, too unlovely. She started to run her hand through her hair, but that would disarrange it. She fretted back and forth across the floor, back and forth, and finally she decided she could put on her negligee and if His Honor walked in on her that was to the better.

She took out not the bright orange one, but the white, lace-trimmed, transparent only here and there, innocent; innocence seemed precious at the moment. She went to the mirror in the bath, wiped off the lipstick and washed her face and did it all over again, in soft pinks and rosy blushes; she felt braver then. But when she came out again to go to bed, there was that black window, void and cold and without any curtain against the night. It was very lonely to sleep in this place. She could not bear to be alone.

And she had slept alone many a night until Tom had come into her life. Tom Ash was a clerk in the Mayor's office in just the next office over from hers; and he was sweet and kind . . . after all, she was beautiful, and still young, only thirty, and seven years she had given to Richard, who was not handsome, though he was attractive after the fashion of older, powerful men; but Tom was . . . Tom was handsome, and a good lover and all those things romances said she was due, and he loved her moreover. He had said so.

Richard did not know about him. Only suspected. Tom had got out the door before Richard arrived, and there was no way in the world Richard could know who it was; more to the point, Richard had asked who it was.

And if Richard had power to put her here despite all the

laws he had power to put Tom here too, and maybe to do worse things.

She was not going to confess to Richard, that was all. She was not going to confess, or she would tell him some other name and let Richard try to figure it all out.

Richard had no proof of anything.

And besides, he did not own her.

Only she liked the good things and the pretty clothes and the nice apartment Tom could never give her. Even her jewelry . . . Richard could figure out a way to take that back. Could blacklist her so she could never find a job, so that she would end up outside the walls, exiled.

She was reading a romance about a woman who had gotten herself into a similar romantic triangle, and it was all too very much like her situation. She was almost afraid to find out how it ended. Light reading. She had always liked light reading, about real, *involved* people, but of a sudden it was much too dramatic and involved her.

But it had to have a happy ending; all such stories did, which was why she kept reading them, to assure herself that she would, and that beautiful women could go on being clever and having happy endings.

Whoever *wanted* tragedy?

She grew weary of reading, having lost the thread of it many times, and arranged the pillows, and having arranged herself as decorously as she could, pushed the light switch by the head of the bed and closed her eyes.

She did sleep a time, more exhausted than she had known, and came to herself with the distinct impression that there had been someone whispering nearby, two someones, in very light voices.

Children, of all things; children in the Tower.

She opened her eyes, gaped upon candlelight, and saw to her wonder two little boys against the brick wall, boys dressed in red and blue brocades, with pale faces, tousled hair and marvelous bright eyes.

"Oh," said one, "she's awake."

"Who are you?" she demanded.

"She's beautiful," said the other. "I wonder if she's nice."

She sat bolt upright, and they held each other as if *she* had frightened them . . . they could hardly be much more than twelve . . . and stared at her wide-eyed.

"Who *are* you?" she asked.

"I'm Edward," said one; "I'm Richard," said the other.

"And how did you get in here?"

Edward let go Richard's arm, pointed vaguely down. "We live here," said young Edward, and part of his hand seemed to go right through the wall.

Then she realized what they must be if they were not a dream, and the hair rose on the back of her neck and she drew the sheet up to cover her, for they *were* children, and she was little covered by the gown. They were quaint and somewhat wise-eyed children, in grown-up clothes which seemed old and dusty.

"How did you get here?" Richard echoed her own question. "Who sent you here? Are you Queen?"

"Richard Collier. The Lord Mayor."

"Ah," said Edward. "A Richard sent us here too. He's supposed to have murdered us both. But he didn't, you know."

She shook her head. She did not know. She never bothered with history. She kept clinging to the idea that they were a dream, some old school lesson come out of her subconscious, for while she believed in ghosts and horoscopes, her mind was reeling under the previous shocks.

"We always come first," said Edward. "I am a king, you know."

"First? What *are* you? What are you doing here?"

"Why, much the same as everyone else," young Edward laughed, and his eyes, while his face was that of a child, now seemed fearsomely old. "We live here, that's all. What's your name?"

"Bettine."

"Bettine? How strange a name. But most are strange now. And so few come here, after all. Do you think he will let you go?"

"Of course he'll let me go."

"Very few ever leave. And no one leaves . . . lately."

"You're dead," she cried. "Go away. Go away."

"We've been dead longer than you've been alive," said Richard.

"Longer than this London's stood here," said Edward. "I liked my London better. It was brighter. I shall always prefer it. Do you play cards?"

She sat and shivered, and Richard tugged at Edward's sleeve.

"I think we should go," said Richard. "I think she's about to be afraid."

"She's very pretty," said Edward. "But I don't think it's going to do her any good."

"It never does," said Richard.

"I go first," said Edward, "being King."

And he vanished, right through the wall; and Richard followed; and the candle glow went out, leaving dark.

Bettine sat still, and held the bedclothes about her, and finally reached for the light button, feverishly, madly, and blinked in the white glare that showed nothing wrong, nothing at all wrong. But there was a deathly chill in the air.

She had dreamed. This strange old place gave her nightmares. It had to be that. Tears ran from her eyes. She shivered and finally she got up and picked at her cold dinner because she wanted something to take her mind off the solitude. She would not look up at the window over the table, not while there was night outside.

She would have shadows beneath her eyes in the morning, and she would not be beautiful, and she had to be. At last she gathered the courage to go back to bed, and lay wrapped in her nightrobe and shivering, in the full light, which she refused to turn out.

She tried the phone again in the morning, and it still refused to work. She found everything saner with the daylight coming in through the window again and the room seemed warmer because of it. She bathed and washed her hair and dried it, brushing it meticulously. It had natural curl and she fashioned it in ringlets and tried it this way and that about her face.

Suddenly the door open on the short hallway closed; she sprang up and looked toward it in consternation, heard footsteps downstairs and dithered about in panic, finally flung on a dress and fluffed her hair and while she heard footsteps coming up the long stairs, leaned near the mirror in the bath and put on her makeup with swift, sure strokes, not the full job, which she had no time for, but at least the touch of definition to the eyes, the blush to lips and cheeks. . . .

It was Richard come to see her, come to ask if she had had enough, and she had, oh, she had. . . .

The far-side door opened. She ran to the door on her side, waited, hands clasped, anxious, meaning to appear anxious and contrite and everything and anything that he should want.

Then the outer door closed again; and hers opened. She rushed to meet her visitor.

There was only a breakfast tray, left on the floor, and the door closed, the footsteps receding.

"Come back!" she cried, wept, wailed.

The steps went on, down the stairs.

She stood there and cried a good long time; and then because she found nothing else to do, she gathered up the tray. She had to bend down to do it, which disarranged her hair and upset her and humiliated her even with no one to see it. She was angry and frightened and wanted to throw the tray and break all the things in sight; but that would make a terrible mess of food and she reckoned that she would have to live in it if she did that, or clean it up herself, so she spared herself such labor and carried it meekly back to the table. She was sick to her stomach, and there was the old food tray which was smelling by now, and the new one which brought new, heavy aromas. She considered them both with her stomach tight with fear and her throat so constricted with anger and frustration that she could not swallow her breaths, let alone the food.

She carried the old tray to the anteroom and set it on the floor, and suddenly, with inspiration, began to search through her belongings for paper . . . she *had* brought some, with the sewing kit, because she made patterns for her embroideries and for her knitting. She searched through the needles and the yarns and found it at the bottom, found the pen, sat down at the desk and chewed the pen's cap, trying to think.

"Richard," she wrote, not "Dearest Richard," which she thought might not be the right approach to an angry man. "I am frightened here. I must see you. Please. Bettine."

That was right, she thought. To be restrained, to be calm, and at the same time dissuade him from doing worse to frighten her. Pathos. That was the tone of it. She folded it up, and with a clever impulse, stitched thread through it to seal it, so that the jailer should not be getting curious without making it obvious. "To His Honor Richard Collier," she wrote on the outside, in the beautiful letters she had practiced making again and again. And then she took it and set it in the supper tray, out in the hall, so that it should leave with the dishes and whoever got it would have to think what to do with it. And throwing away a letter to the Mayor was not a wise thing to do.

She sniffed then, satisfied, and sat down and ate her breakfast, which did fill a little bit of the loneliness in her stomach, and made her feel guilty and miserable afterward, because she had eaten too much; she would get fat, that was what they wanted, feeding her all that and leaving her nothing to do but eat; she would soon be fat and unlovely if there was nothing to do here but eat and pace the floor.

And maybe she would be here a long time. That began to penetrate her with a force it had not until now. A second day in this place . . . and how many days; and she would run out of things to read and to do . . . she set the second tray in the hall too, to be rid of the smell of the food, and punched buttons trying to close the door from inside; the whole console was complicated, and she started punching buttons at random. There were controls she did not know; she punched buttons in different combinations and only succeeded in getting the lights out in a way in which she could not get them on again, not from any combination of buttons until finally she punched the one by the bed. That frightened her, that she might cut off the heating or lose the lighting entirely and be alone in the dark when the sun should go down. She stopped punching buttons, knowing nothing of what she was doing with them, although when she had been in school there had been a course in managing the computers . . . but that was something the other girls did, who had plain long faces and fastened their hair back and had flat bodies and thought of nothing but studying and working. She hated them. Hated the whole thing. Hated prisons that could be made of such things.

She picked up her knitting and thought of Tom, of his eyes, his body, his voice . . . he *loved* her; and Richard did not, perhaps, but used her because she was beautiful, and one had to put up with that. It brought things. Would buy her way out of here. Richard might be proud and angry and have his feelings hurt, but ultimately he would want his pride salved, and she could do that, abundantly, assuring him that she was contrite, which was all she had to do, ultimately.

It was Tom she daydreamed of, wondering where he was and if he was in the Tower too. Oh, surely, surely not; but the books she read seemed so frighteningly real, and dire things happened for jealousy. She began to think of Tom in that kind of trouble, while her hands plied the colored yarns, knitting click, click, click, measuring out the time, stitch by stitch and row by row. Women did such things and went on doing them while the sun died because in all of women's lives there were so many moments that would kill the mind if one thought about them, which would suck the heart and the life out of one, and engrave lines in the face and put gray in the hair if ever one let one's mind work; but there was in the rhythm and the fascination of the stitches a loss of thought, a void, a blank, that was only numbers and not even that, because the mind did not need to count, the fingers did, the length of a thread against the finger measured evenly as a ruler could divide it, the slight difference in tension sensed finely as a machine could sense, the exact *number* of stitches keeping pattern without really the need to count, but something inward and regular as the beat of a heart, as the slow passing of time which could be frozen in such acts, or speeded past.

So the day passed; and click, click, click the needles went, using up the yarn, when she did not read; and she wound more and knitted more, row upon row, not thinking.

There was no noon meal; the sun began to fade, and the room grew more chill. I shall have to ask for more yarn someday, she thought with surprising placidity, and realized what that thought implied and refused to think anymore. At last she heard the steps coming up to the door and this time she refused to spring up and expect it to be Richard. She went right on with her knitting, click, click, while the steps came up and opened the door and closed it again.

Then quite calmly she went out and retrieved the new tray, saw with a little surge of hope that the message and the trays had gone. So, she thought; so, it will get to him; and she sat down and had her dinner, but not all of it. She took the tray out to the anteroom after, and went back and prepared herself for bed.

The light faded from the window, and the outside became black again; again she avoided looking toward it, because it so depressed her, and made the little room on the third level so lonely and so isolated.

And again she went to bed with the light on, because she was not willing to suffer more such illusions . . . they *were* illusions, and she put her mind from them all day long. She *believed* in supernatural things, but it had stopped being something which happened to someone else, and something

which waited to happen to her, which was not shivery-enter-
taining, not in the least. It rather made her fear she was losing touch with things and losing control of her imagination,
and she refused to have that happen.

She put on her white negligee again, reckoning that she
just could be summoned out of bed by a phone call . . . after all, the message *could* be carried to His Honor Richard
Collier direct. But it was more likely that it would go to his
office instead, and that the call would come tomorrow, so she
could relax just a bit and get some sleep, which she really
needed. She was not actually afraid this second night, and so
long as lights were on, there was no likelihood that she would
have silly dreams about dead children.

Dead children. She shuddered, appalled that such a dream
could have come out of her own imagination; it was not at
all the kind of thing that a girl wanted to think about.

Tom . . . now *he* was worth thinking about.

She read her story; and the woman in the story had prob-
lems *not* direr than hers, which made her own seem worse
and the story seem trivial; but it was going to be a happy
ending. She was sure that it would, which would cheer her
up.

Would they give her more books, she wondered, when
these ran out? She thought that in the morning she would put
another note on the tray and ask for books for herself; and
maybe she should not, because that would admit to the jailer
that she thought she was staying; and *that* would get to
Richard too, who would ask how she was bearing up. She
was sure that he would ask.

No. She would not ask for things to indicate a long stay
here. They might give them to her, and she could not bear
that.

Again she found she was losing the thread of the story,
and she laid the book down against the side of the bed. She
tried to think of Tom and could not, losing the thread of him
too. She dreamed only the needles, back and forth, in and
out, click.

The light dimmed . . . to candlelight; she felt it dim
through her closed lids; and she cracked a lid very carefully,
her muscles rigid and near to shivering. The dream was back;
she heard the children laughing together.

"Well," said Edward's voice, "hello, Bettine."

She looked; she had to, not knowing how near they were,

afraid they might touch her. They were standing against the bricks again, both of them, solemn-faced like boys holding some great joke confined for the briefest of moments.

"Of course we're back," said the boy Richard. "How are you, lady Bettine?"

"Go away," she said; and then the least little part of her heart said that she did not really want them to go. She blinked and sat up, and there was a woman walking toward her out of the wall, who became larger and larger as the boys retreated. The newcomer was beautiful, in an ancient mode, wearing a golden brocade gown. The visitor dipped a curtsy to the boy king Edward, who bowed to her. "Madam," the boy-king said; and "Majesty," said the stranger, and turned curious eyes on *her.* "She is Bettine," said Edward. "Be polite, Bettine: Anne is one of the queens."

"Queen Anne?" asked Bettine, wishing that she knew a little more of the ancient Tower. If one was to be haunted, it would be at least helpful to know by whom; but she had paid very little attention to history—there was so much of it.

"Boleyn," said the queen, and spread her skirts and sat on the end of her bed, narrowly missing her feet, very forthright for a dream. "And how are you, my dear?"

"Very well, thank you, Majesty."

The boys laughed. "She only half believes in us, but she plays the game, doesn't she? They don't have queens now."

"How pretty she is," said the queen. "So was I."

"I'm not staying here," Bettine said. It seemed important in this web of illusions to have that clear. "I don't really believe in you entirely. I'm dreaming this anyway."

"You're not, my dear, but there, there, believe what you like." The queen turned, looked back; the children had gone, and another was coming through, a handsome man in elegant brocade. "Robert Devereaux," said Anne. "Robert, her name is Bettine."

"Who is he?" Bettine asked. "Is he the king?"

The man named Robert laughed gently and swept a bow; "I might have been," he said. "But things went wrong."

"Earl of Essex," said Anne softly, and stood up and took his hand. "The boys said that there was someone who believed in us, all the same. How nice. It's been so long."

"You make me very nervous," she said. "If you were real I think you'd talk differently; something old. You're just like me."

Robert laughed. "But we aren't like the walls, Bettine. We do change. We listen and we learn and we watch all the passing time."

"Even the children," said Anne.

"You died here."

"Indeed we did. And the same way."

"Murdered?" she asked with a shiver.

Anne frowned. "Beheaded, my dear. Quite a few had a hand in arranging it. I was maneuvered, you see; and how should I know we were spied on?"

"You and Essex?"

"Ah, no," said Robert. "*We* weren't lovers, then."

"Only now," said Anne. "We met . . . posthumously on my part. And how are you here, my dear?"

"I'm the Mayor's girl," Bettine said. It was good to talk, to have even shadows to talk to. She sat forward, embracing her knees in her arms. Suddenly the tears began to flow, and she daubed at her eyes with the sheet, feeling a little silly to be talking to ectoplasms, which all the fashionable folk denied existed; and yet it helped. "We quarreled and he put me here."

"Oh dear," said Anne.

"Indeed," said Lord Essex, patting Anne's hand. "That's why the boys said we should come. It's very like us."

"You died for love?"

"Politics," said Anne. "So will you."

She shook her head furiously. This dream of hers was not in her control, and she tried to drag things her own way. "But it's a silly quarrel. And I don't die. They don't kill people here, they don't."

"They do," Anne whispered. "Just like they did."

"Well," said Essex, "not axes, any more. They're much neater than they were."

"Go away," Bettine cried. "Go away, go away, go away."

"You'd do well to talk with us," said Anne. "We could make you understand what you're really up against. And there's really so much you don't seem to see, Bettine."

"Don't think of love," said Essex. "It's not love, you know, that sends people here. It's only politics. I know that. And Anne does. Besides, you don't sound like someone in love, do you? You don't sound like someone in love, Bettine."

She shrugged and looked down, expecting that they would be gone when she looked up. "There *is* someone I love," she said in the faintest of whispers when she saw they were not gone.

Anne snorted delicately. "That's not worth much here. Eternity is long, Bettine. And there's love and love, Bettine." She wound insubstantial fingers with the earl's. "You mustn't think of it being love. That's not the reason you'.e here. Be wise, Bettine. These stones have seen a great deal come and go. So have we; and you don't have the face of one who loves."

"What do *you* know?" she cried. "You're nothing. I know *people*, believe me. And I know Richard."

"Good night, Bettine," Anne said.

"Good night," Essex said very softly and patiently, so that she did not seem to have ruffled either of them at all. And the children were back, who bowed with departing irony and faded. The lights brightened.

She flounced down among the bedclothes sulking at such depressing ideas and no small bit frightened, but not of the ghosts—of her situation. Of things they said. There was a chill in the air, and a whiff of dried old flowers and spices . . . the flowers, she thought, was Anne; and the spice must be Essex. Or maybe it was the children Edward and Richard. The apparitions did not threaten her; they only spoke her fears. That was what they really were, after all. Ectoplasms, indeed. She burrowed into the covers and punched out the lights, having dispensed with fear of ghosts; her eyes hurt and she was tired. She lay down with utter abandon, which she had really not done since she came, burrowed among the pillows and tried not to think or dream at all.

In the morning the phone came on and the screen lit up.

"Bettine," said Richard's voice, stern and angry.

She sprang up out of the covers, went blank for a moment and then assumed one of her bedroom looks, pushed her thick masses of hair looser on her head, stood up with a sinuous twist of her body and looked into the camera, moue'd into a worried frown, a tremble, a look near tears.

"Richard. Richard, I was so afraid. Please." Keep him feeling superior, keep him feeling great and powerful, which was what she was *for* in the world, after all, and how she lived. She came and stood before the camera, leaned there. "I want out of here, Richard. I don't understand this place." Naïveté always helped, helplessness; and it was, besides, truth. "The jailer was terrible." Jealousy, if she could provoke it. "Please, let me come back. I never meant to do anything wrong . . . what is it I've *done,* Richard?"

"Who was he?"

Her heart was beating very fast. Indignation now; set him off balance. "No one. I mean, it was just a small thing and he wasn't anyone in particular, and I never did anything like that before, Richard, but you left me alone and what's a girl to do, after all? Two weeks and you hadn't called me or talked to me—?"

"What's the *name,* Bettine? And where's the grade-fifty file? Where is it, Bettine?"

She was the one off balance. She put a shaking hand to her lips, blinked, shook her head in real disorganization. "I don't know anything about the file." This wasn't it, this wasn't what it was supposed to be about. "Honestly, Richard, I don't know. What file? Is *that* what this is? That you think I *stole* something? Richard, I never, I never stole anything."

"Someone got into the office. Someone who didn't belong there, Bettine; and you have the key, and I do, and that's a pretty limited range, isn't it? My office. My private office. Who did that, Bettine?"

"I don't know," she wailed, and pushed her hair aside—the pretty gestures were lifelong-learned and automatic. "Richard, I've gotten caught in something I don't understand at all, I don't understand, I don't, and I never let anyone in there." (But Tom had gotten in there; *he* could have, any time, since he was in the next office.) "Maybe the door . . . maybe I left it open and I shouldn't have, but, Richard, I don't even know what was in that file, I swear I don't."

"Who was in your apartment that night?"

"I—it wasn't connected to that, it wasn't, Richard, and I wish you'd understand that. It wasn't anything, but that I was lonely and it was a complete mistake, and now if I gave you somebody's name then it would get somebody in trouble who just never was involved; I mean, I might have been careless, Richard, I guess I was; I'm terribly sorry about the file, but I did leave the door open sometimes, and you were gone a lot. I mean . . . it was possible someone could have gotten in there, but you never told me there was any kind of trouble like that. . . ."

"The access numbers. You understand?"

"I don't. I never saw that file."

"Who was in your apartment?"

She remained silent, thinking of Tom, and her lip trembled. It went on trembling while Richard glared at her, because she could not make up her mind what she ought to do and what was safe. She could *handle* Richard. She was sure that she could.

And then he blinked out on her.

"Richard!" she screamed. She punched buttons in vain. The screen was dead. She paced the floor and wrung her hands and stared out the window.

She heard the guard coming, and her door closed and the outer door opened for the exchange of the tray. Then the door gave back again and she went out into the anteroom after it. She carried the tray back and set it on the table, finally went to the bath and looked at herself, at sleep-tangled hair and shadowed eyes and the stain of old cosmetic. She was appalled at the face she had shown to Richard, at what she had been surprised into showing him. She scrubbed her face at once and brushed her hair and put slippers on her bare feet, which were chilled to numbness on the tiles.

Then she ate her breakfast, sparingly, careful of her figure, and dressed and sat and sewed. The silence seemed twice as heavy as before. She hummed to herself and tried to fill the void. She sang—she had a beautiful voice, and she sang until she feared she would grow hoarse, while the pattern grew. She read some of the time, and, bored, she found a new way to do her hair; but then she thought after she had done it that if Richard should call back he might not like it, and it was important that he like the way she looked. She combed it back the old way, all the while mistrusting this instinct, this reliance on a look which had already failed.

So the day passed, and Richard did not call again.

They wanted Tom. There was the chance that if she did give Richard Tom's name it could be the right one, because it was all too obvious who *could* have gotten a file out of Richard's office, because there had been many times Richard had been gone and Tom had followed her about her duties, teasing her.

Safest not to ask and not to know. She was determined not to. She resented the thing that had happened—politics—politics. She hated politics.

Tom . . . was someone to love. Who loved her; and Richard had reasons which were Richard's, but it came down to two men being jealous. And Tom, being innocent, had no idea what he was up against . . . Tom could be hurt, but Richard would never hurt her; and while she did not tell Richard, she still had the power to perplex him. While he was perplexed he would do nothing.

She was not totally confident . . . of Tom's innocence, or of Richard's attitude. She was not accustomed to saying no. She was not accustomed to being put in difficult positions. Tom should not have asked it of her. He should have known. It was not fair what he did, whatever he had gotten himself involved in—some petty little record-juggling—to have put her in this position.

The pattern grew, delicate rows of stitches, complex designs which needed no thinking, only seeing, and she wept sometimes and wiped at her eyes while she worked.

Light faded from the window. Supper came and she ate, and this night she did not prepare for bed, but wrapped her night robe about her for warmth and sat in the chair and waited, lacking all fear, expecting the children, looking forward to them in a strangely keen longing, because they were at least company, and laughter was good to hear in this grim place. Even the laughter of murdered children.

There began to be a great stillness. And not the laughter of children this time, but the tread of heavier feet, the muffled clank of metal. A grim, shadowed face materialized in dimming light.

She stood up, alarmed, and warmed her chilling hands before her lips. "Edward," she cried aloud. "Edward, Richard . . . are you there?" But what was coming toward her was taller and bare of face and arm and leg, bronze elsewhere, and wearing a *sword*, of all things. She wanted the children; wanted Anne or Robert Devereaux, any of the others. This one . . . was different.

"Bettine," he said in a voice which echoed in far distances. "Bettine."

"I don't think I like you," she said.

The ghost stopped with a little clank of armor, kept fading in and out. He was young, even handsome in a foreign way. He took off his helmet and held it under his arm. "I'm Marc," he said. "Marcus Atilius Regulus. They said I should come. Could you see your way, Bettine, to prick your finger?"

"Why should I do that?"

"I am oldest," he said. "Well—almost, and of a different

persuasion, and perhaps it is old-fashioned, but it would make our speaking easier."

She picked up her sewing needle and jabbed her cold finger, once and hard, and the blood welled up black in the dim light and fell onto the stones. She put the injured finger in her mouth, and stared quite bewildered, for the visitor was very much brighter, and seemed to draw a living breath.

"Ah," he said. "Thank you with all my heart, Bettine."

"I'm not sure at all I should have done that. I think you might be dangerous."

"Ah, no, Bettine."

"Were you a soldier, some kind of knight?"

"A soldier, yes; and a knight, but not the kind you think of. I think you mean of the kind born to this land. I came from Tiberside. I am Roman, Bettine. We laid some of the oldest stones just . . ." he lifted a braceletted arm, rather confusedly toward one of the steel walls. "But most of the old work is gone now. There are older levels; all the surly ones tend to gather down there. Even new ones, and some that never were civilized, really, or never quite accepted being dead, all of them—" he made a vague and deprecating gesture. "But we don't get many now, because there hasn't been anyone in here who could believe in us . . . in so very long . . . does the finger hurt?"

"No." She sucked at it and rubbed the moisture off and looked at him more closely. "I'm not sure *I* believe in you."

"You're not sure you don't, and that's enough."

"Why are you here? Where are the others?"

"Oh, they're back there."

"But why you? Why wouldn't they come? I expected the children."

"Oh. They're there. Nice boys."

"And why did *you* come? What has a soldier to do with me?"

"I—come for the dead. I'm the psychopomp."

"The what?"

"Psychopomp. Soul-guider. When you die."

"But I'm not going to die," she wailed, hugging her arms about her and looking without wanting to at the ancient sword he wore. "There's a mistake, that's all. I've been trying to explain to the others, but they don't understand. We're civilized. We don't go around killing people in here, whatever *used* to happen. . . ."

"Oh, they *do*, Bettine; but we don't get them, because they're very stubborn, and they believe in nothing, and they can't see us. Last month I lost one. I almost had him to see me, but at the last he just couldn't; and he slipped away and I'm not sure where. It looked hopelessly drear. I try with all of them. I'm glad you're not like them."

"But you're wrong. I'm not going to die."

He shrugged, and his dark eyes looked very sad.

"I can get out of here," she said, unnerved at his lack of belief in her. "If I have to, there's always a way. I can just tell them what they want to know and they'll let me go."

"Ah," he said.

"It's true."

His young face, so lean and serious, looked sadder still. "Oh Bettine."

"It *is* true; what do *you* know?"

"Why haven't you given them what they want before now?"

"Because. . . ." She made a gesture to explain and then shook her head. "Because I think I can get out of it without doing that."

"For pride? Or for honor?"

It sounded like something *he* should say, after all, all done up in ancient armor and carrying a sword. "You've been dead a long time," she said.

"Almost the longest of all. *Superbia*, we said. That's the wrong kind of pride; that's being puffed up and too important and not really seeing things right. And there's *exemplum*. That's a thing you do because the world needs it, like setting up something for people to look at, a little marker, to say Marcus Regulus stood here."

"And what if no one sees it? What good is it then, if I never get out of here? There's being brave and being stupid."

He shook his head very calmly. "An *exemplum* is an *exemplum* even if no one sees it. They're just markers, where someone was."

"Look outside, old ghost. The sun's going out and the world's dying."

"Still," he said, "*exempla* last . . . because there's nothing anyone can do to erase them."

"What, like old stones?"

"No. Just moments. Moments are the important thing. Not every moment, but more than some think."

"Well," she said, perplexed and bothered. "Well, that's all very well for men who go around fighting ancient wars, but I don't fight anyone. I don't like violence at all, and I'll do what I can for Tom but I'm not brave and there's a limit."

"Where, Bettine?"

"The next time Richard asks me, that's where. I want out of here."

He looked sad.

"Stop that," she snapped. "I suppose you think you're superior."

"No."

"I'm just a girl who has to live and they can take my job away and I can end up outside the walls starving, that's what could happen to me."

"Yes, sometimes *exempla* just aren't quick. Mine would have been. And I failed it."

"You're a soldier. I'm a woman."

"Don't you think about honor at all, Bettine?"

"You're out of date. I stopped being a virgin when I was thirteen."

"No. *Honor*, Bettine."

"I'll bet you were some kind of hero, weren't you, some old war hero?"

"Oh no, Bettine. I wasn't. I ran away. That's why I'm the psychopomp. Because the old Tower's a terrible place; and a good many of the dead do break down as they die. There were others who could have taken the job: the children come first, usually, just to get the prisoners used to the idea of ghosts, but I come at the last . . . because I know what it is to be afraid, and what it is to want to run. I'm an Atilius Regulus, and there were heroes in my house, oh, there was a great one . . . I could tell you the story. I will, someday. But in the same family there was myself, and they were never so noble after me. *Exemplum* had something to do with it. I wish I could have left a better one. It came on me so quickly . . . a moment; one lives all one's life to be ready for moments when they come. I used to tell myself, you know, that if mine had just—crept up slowly, then I should have thought it out; I always did think. But I've seen so much, so very much, and I know human beings, and do you know . . . quick or slow in coming, it was what I *was* that made the difference, thinking or not; and I just wasn't then what I am now."

"Dead," she said vengefully.

He laughed silently. "And eons wiser." Then his face went sober. "O Bettine, courage comes from being ready whenever the moment comes, not with the mind . . . I don't think anyone ever is. But what you *are* . . . can be ready."

"What happened to you?"

"I was an officer, you understand. . . ." He gestured at the armor he wore. "And when the Britons got over the rampart . . . I ran, and took all my unit with me—I didn't think what I was doing; *I* was getting clear. But a wise old centurion met me coming his way and ran me through right there. The men stopped running then and put the enemy back over the wall, indeed they did. And a lot of men were saved and discipline held. So I was an *exemplum*, after all; even if I was someone else's. It hurt. I don't mean the wound—those never do quite the way you think, I can tell you that—but I mean really hurt, so that it was a long long time before I came out in the open again—after the Tower got to be a prison. After I saw so many lives pass here. Then I decided I should come out. May I touch you?"

She drew back, bumped the chair, shivered. "That's not how you. . . ?"

"O no. *I* don't take lives. May I touch you?"

She nodded mistrustingly, kept her eyes wide open as he drifted nearer and a braceletted hand came toward her face, beringed and masculine and only slightly transparent. It was like a breath of cool wind, and his young face grew wistful. Because she was beautiful, she thought, with a little rush of pride, and he was young and very handsome and very long dead.

She wondered. . . .

"Warmth," he said, his face very near and his dark eyes very beautiful. "I had gone into my melancholy again . . . in all these last long centuries, that there was no more for me to do, no souls for me to meet, no special one who believed, no one at all. I thought it was all done. Are there more who still believe?"

"Yes," she said. And started, for there were Anne and Essex holding hands within the brickwork or behind it or somewhere; and other shadowy figures. The children were there, and a man who looked very wet, with a slight reek of alcohol, and more and more and more, shadows which went from brocades to metals to leather to furs and strange helmets.

"Go away," she cried at that flood, and fled back, overturning the tray and crowding into the corner. "Get out of here. I'm not going to die. I'm not brave and I'm not going to. Let someone else do the dying. I don't want to die."

They murmured softly and faded; and there came a touch at her cheek like a cool breeze.

"Go away!" she shrieked, and she was left with only the echoes. "I'm going mad," she said then to herself, and dropped into the chair and bowed her head into her hands. When she finally went to bed she sat fully dressed in the corner and kept the lights on.

Breakfast came, and she bathed and dressed, and read her book, which began to come to its empty and happy ending. She threw it aside, because her life was not coming out that way, and she kept thinking of Tom, and crying, not sobs, just a patient slow leaking of tears, which made her makeup run and kept her eyes swollen. She was not powerful. She had lost all illusion of that. She just wanted out of this alive, and to live and to forget it. She tried again to use the phone and she could not figure out the keyboard which she thought might give her access to *someone,* if she knew anything about such systems, and she did not.

For the first time she became convinced that she was in danger of dying here, and that instead, Tom was going to, and she would be in a way responsible. She was no one, no one against all the anger that swirled about her. She was quite, quite helpless; and not brave at all, and nothing in her life had ever prepared her to be. She thought back to days when she was a child, and in school, and all kinds of knowledge had been laid out in front of her. She had found it useless . . . which it was, to a ten-year-old girl who thought she had the world all neatly wrapped around her finger. Who thought at that age that she knew all the things that were important, that if she went on pleasing others that the world would always be all right.

Besides, the past was about dead people and she liked living ones; and learning about science was learning that the world was in the process of ending, and there was no cheer in that. She wanted to be Bettine Maunfry who had all that she would ever need. Never think, never think about days too far ahead, or things too far to either side, or understand things, which made it necessary to decide, and prepare.

Moments. She had never wanted to imagine such moments would come. There was no time she could have looked down the long currents of her life, which had *not* been so long after all, and when she could have predicted that Bettine Maunfry would have gotten herself into a situation like this. People were supposed to take care of her. There had always been someone to take care of her. That was what it was being female and beautiful and young. It was just not supposed to happen this way.

Tom, she thought. O Tom, now what do I do, what am I supposed to do?

But of course the doing was hers.

To him.

She had no idea what her horoscope or his was on this date, but she thought that it must be disaster, and she fingered the little fishes which she wore still in her décolletage for His Honor Richard Collier to see.

And she waited, to bend as she had learned to bend; only . . . she began to think with the versatility of the old Bettine . . . never give up an advantage. *Never*.

She went in and washed her face and put on her makeup again, and stopped her crying and repaired all the subtle damages of her tears.

She dressed in her handsomest dress and waited.

And toward sundown the call came.

"Bettine," His Honor said. "Have you thought better of it, Bettine?"

She came and faced the screen and stood there with her lips quivering and her chin trembling because weakness worked for those who knew how to use it.

"I might," she said.

"There's no 'might' about it, Bettine," said Richard Collier, his broad face suffused with red. "Either you do or you don't."

"When you're here," she said, "when you come here and see me yourself, I'll tell you."

"Before I come."

"No," she said, letting the tremor become very visible. "I'm *afraid*, Richard; I'm afraid. If you'll come here and take me out of here yourself, I promise I'll tell you anything I know,

which isn't much, but I'll tell you. I'll give you his name, but
he's not involved with anything besides that he had a silly in-
fatuation and I was lonely. But I won't tell anything if you
don't come and get me out of here. This has gone far
enough, Richard. I'm frightened. Bring me home."

He stared at her, frowning. "If I come over there and you
change your mind, Bettine, you can forget any favors you
think I owe you. I won't be played with. You understand me,
girl?"

She nodded.

"All right," he said. "You'll tell me his name, and you'll be
thinking up any other detail that might explain how he could
have gotten to that office, and you do it tonight. I'm sure
there's some sense in that pretty head, there's a girl. You just
think about it, Bettine, and you think hard, and where you
want to be. Home, with all the comforts . . . or where you
are, which isn't comfortable at all, is it, Bettine?"

"No," she said, crying. She shook her head. "No. It's not
comfortable, Richard."

"See you in the morning, Bettine. And you can pack, if
you have the right name."

"Richard——" But he had winked out, and she leaned there
against the wall shivering, with her hands made into fists and
the feeling that she was very small indeed. She did not want
to be in the Tower another night, did not want to face the
ghosts, who would stare at her with sad eyes and talk to her
about honor, about things that were not for Bettine Maunfry.

I'm sorry, she thought for them. I won't be staying and dying here after all.

But Tom would. That thought depressed her enormously.
She felt somehow responsible, and that was a serious burden,
more serious than anything she had ever gotten herself into
except the time she had thought for ten days that she was
pregnant. Maybe Tom would—lie to them; maybe Tom
would try to tell them she was somehow to blame in something which was not her fault.

That frightened her. But Tom loved her. He truly did.
Tom would not hurt her by anything he would say, being a
man, and braver, and motivated by some vaguely different
drives, which had to do with pride and being strong, qualities
which she had avoided all her life.

She went through the day's routines, such of the day as

was left, and packed all but her dress that Richard said matched her eyes. She put that one on, to sit up all the night, because she was determined that Richard should not surprise her looking other than beautiful, and it would be like him to try that mean trick. She would simply sleep sitting up and keep her skirts from wrinkling, all propped with pillows: that way she could both be beautiful and get some sleep.

And she kept the lights on because of the ghosts, who were going to feel cheated.

Had he really died that way, she wondered of the Roman, the young Roman, who talked about battles from forgotten ages. Had he really died that way or did he only make it up to make her listen to him? She thought about battles which might have been fought right where this building stood, all the many, many ages.

And the lights faded.

The children came, grave and sober, Edward and then Richard, who stood and stared with liquid, disapproving eyes.

"I'm sorry," she said shortly. "I'm going to be leaving."

The others then, Anne and Robert, Anne with her heart-shaped face and dark hair and lovely manners, Essex tall and elegant, neither looking at her quite the way she expected— not disapproving, more as if they had swallowed secrets. "It was politics after all," asked Anne, "wasn't it, Bettine?"

"Maybe it was," she said shortly, hating to be proved wrong. "But what's that to me? I'm still getting out of here."

"What if your lover accuses you?" asked Essex. "Loves do end."

"He won't," she said. "He wouldn't. He's not likely to."

"*Exemplum*," said a mournful voice. "O Bettine, is this yours?"

"Shut up," she told Marc. He was hardest to face, because his sad, dark gaze seemed to expect something special of her. She was instantly sorry to have been rude; he looked as if his heart was breaking. He wavered, and she saw him covered in dust, the armor split, and bloody, and tears washing down his face. She put her hands to her face, horrified.

"You've hurt him," said Anne. "We go back to the worst moment when we're hurt like that."

"O Marc," she said, "I'm sorry. I don't want to hurt you. But I want to be *alive*, you understand . . . can't you remember that? Wouldn't you have traded anything for that? And you had so much . . . when the sun was young and everything was new. O Marc, do you blame me?"

"There is only one question," he said, his eyes melting-sad. "It's your moment, Bettine. Your moment."

"Well, I'm not like you; I never was; never will be. What good is being right and dead? And what's right? Who's to know? It's all relative. Tom's not that wonderful, I'll have you to know. And neither's Richard. And a girl gets along the best she can."

A wind blew, and there was a stirring among the others, an intaken breath. Essex caught at Anne's slim form, and the children withdrew to Anne's skirts. "It's *her*," said young Edward. "*She's* come."

Only Marc refused the panic which took the others; bright again, he moved with military precision to one side, cast a look back through the impeding wall where a tiny figure advanced.

"She didn't die here," he said quietly. "But she has many ties to this place. She is one of the queens, Bettine, a great one. And very seldom does *she* come out."

"For me?"

"Because you are one of the last, perhaps."

She shook her head, looked again in bewilderment as Anne and Robert and young Richard bowed; and Edward inclined his head. Marc only touched his heart and stepped further aside. "Marc," Bettine protested, not wanting to lose him, the one she trusted.

"Well," said the visitor, a voice like the snap of ice. She seemed less woman than small monument, in a red and gold gown covered with embroideries and pearls, and ropes of pearls and pearls in crisp red hair; she had a pinched face out of which two eyes stared like living cinder. "Well?"

Bettine bowed like the others; she thought she ought. The Queen paced slowly, diverted herself for a look at Essex, and a slow nod at Anne. "Well."

"My daughter," said Anne. "The first Elizabeth."

"Indeed," said the Queen. "And Marc, good evening. Marc, how do you fare? And the young princes. Quite a stir, my dear, indeed quite a stir you've made. I have my spies; no need to reiterate."

"I'm not dying," she said. "You're all mistaken. I've told them I'm not dying. I'm going back to Richard."

The Queen looked at Essex, offered her hand. Essex kissed it, held it, smiled wryly. "Didn't you once say something of the kind?" asked the Queen.

"He did," said Anne. "It was, after all, your mistake, daughter."

"At the time," said Elizabeth. "But it was very stupid of you, Robert, to have relied on old lovers as messengers."

Essex shrugged, smiled again. "If not that year, the next. We were doomed to disagree."

"Of course," Elizabeth said. "There's love and there's power; and we all three wanted that, didn't we? And you . . ." Again that burning look turned on Bettine. "What sort are you? Not a holder. A seeker after power?"

"Neither one. I'm the Lord Mayor's girl and I'm going home."

"The Lord Mayor's girl." Elizabeth snorted. "The Lord Mayor's girl. I have spies, I tell you; all London's haunted. I've asked questions. The fellow gulled you, this Tom Ash. Ah, he himself's nothing; he works for others. He needs the numbers, that's all, for which he's paid. And with that list in others' hands your precious Lord Mayor's in dire trouble. Revolution, my dear, the fall of princes. Are you so blind? Your Lord Mayor's none so secure, tyrant that he is . . . if not this group of men, this year, then others, next. They'll have him; London town's never cared for despots, crowned or plain. Not even in its old age has it grown soft-witted. Just patient."

"I don't want to hear any of it. Tom loved me, that's all. Whatever he's involved in . . ."

Elizabeth laughed. "I was born to power. Was it accident? Ask my mother here what she paid. Ask Robert here what he paid to try for mine, and how I held it all the same . . . no hard feelings, none. But do you think your Lord Mayor gained his by accident? You move in dark waters, with your eyes *shut*. You've wanted power all your life, and you thought there was an easy way. But you don't have it, because you don't understand what you want. If they gave you all of London on a platter, you'd see only the baubles. You'd look for some other hands to put the real power in; you're helpless. You've trained all your life to be, I'll warrant. I know the type. Bettine. What name is that? Abbreviated and diminished. *E-liz-a-beth* is our name, in fine round tones. You're

tall; you try to seem otherwise. You dress to please everyone
else; I pleased *Elizabeth,* and others copied me. If I was fond,
it was that I liked men, but by all reason, I never handed my
crown to one, no. However painful the decision . . . however
many the self-serving ministers urging me this way and that, I
did my own thinking; yes, Essex, even with you. Of course
I'd hesitate, of course let the ministers urge me, of course I'd
grieve—I'm not unhuman—but at the same time they could
seem heartless and I merciful. And the deed got done, didn't
it, Robert?"

"Indeed," he said.

"You were one of my favorites; much as you did, I always
liked you; loved you, of course, but liked you, and there
weren't as many of those. And you, Mother, another of the
breed. But this modern bearer of my name—you have none
of it, no backbone at all."

"I'm not in your class," Bettine said. "It's not fair."

"Whine and whimper. You're a born victim. I could make
you a queen and you'd be a dead one in a fortnight."

"I just want to be comfortable and I want to be happy."

"Well, look at you."

"I will be again. I'm not going to be dead; I'm going to get
out of this."

"Ah. You want, want, want; never look to see how things
are. You spend all your life reacting to what others do. Ever
thought about getting in the first stroke? No, of course not.
I'm Elizabeth. You're just Bettine."

"I wasn't born with your advantages."

Elizabeth laughed. "I was a bastard . . . pardon me,
Mother. And what were you? Why aren't *you* the Mayor?
Ever wonder that?"

Bettine turned away, lips trembling.

"Look at me," said the Queen.

She did so, not wanting to. But the voice was commanding.

"Why did you?"

"What?"

"Look at me."

"You asked."

"Do you do everything people ask? You're everyone's victim, that's all. The Mayor's girl. You choose to be, no getting
out of it. You *choose,* even by choosing not to choose. You'll
go back and you'll give His Honor what he wants, and you'll
go back to your apartment . . . maybe."

"What do you mean maybe?"

"Think, my girl, think. Girl you are; you've spent your whole majority trying to be nothing. I think you may achieve it."

"There's the Thames," said Essex.

"It's not what they take from you," said Anne, "it's what you give up."

"The water," said Edward, "is awfully cold, so I've heard."

"What do you know? You didn't have any life."

"But I did," said the boy, his eyes dancing. "I had my years . . . like you said, when the sun was very good."

"I had a pony," said Richard. "Boys don't, now."

"Be proud," said Elizabeth.

"I know something about you," Bettine said. "You got old and you had no family and no children, and I'm sure pride was cold comfort then."

Elizabeth smiled. "I hate to disillusion you, my dear, but I *was* happy. Ah, I shed a few tears, who doesn't in a lifetime? But I had exactly what I chose; and what I traded I knew I traded. I did precisely as I wanted. Not always the story book I would have had it, but for all that, within my circumstances, precisely as I chose, for all my life to its end. I lived and I was curious; there was nothing I thought foreign to me. I saw more of the world in a glance than you've wondered about lifelong. I was ahead of my times, never caught by the outrageously unanticipated; but your whole life's an accident, isn't it, little Elizabeth?"

"Bettine," she said, setting her chin. "My *name* is Bettine."

"Good," laughed the Queen, slapping her skirted thigh. "Excellent. Go *on* thinking; and straighten your back, woman. Look at the eyes. Always look at the eyes."

The Queen vanished in a little thunderclap, and Essex swore and Anne patted his arm. "She was never comfortable," Anne said. "I would have brought her up with gentler manners."

"If I'd been your son—" said Essex.

"If," said Anne.

"They'll all be disturbed downstairs," said young Edward. "They *are*, when she comes through."

They faded . . . all but Marc.

"They don't change my mind," said Bettine. "The Queen was rude."

"No," said Marc. "Queens aren't. She's just what she is."

"Rude," she repeated, still smarting.

"Be what you are," said Marc, "I'll go. It's your moment."

"Marc?" She reached after him, forgetting. Touched nothing. She was alone then, and it was too quiet. She would have wanted Marc to stay. Marc understood fear.

Be what she was. She laughed sorrowfully, wiped at her eyes, and went to the bath to begin to be beautiful, looked at eyes which had puffed and which were habitually reddened from want of sleep. And from crying. She found herself crying now, and did not know why, except maybe at the sight of Bettine Maunfry as she was, little slim hands that had never done anything and a face which was all sex and a voice that no one would ever obey or take seriously . . . just for games, was Bettine. In all this great place which had held desperate criminals and fallen queens and heroes and lords, just Bettine, who was going to do the practical thing and turn in Tom who had never loved her, but only wanted something.

Tom's another, she thought with curiously clear insight, a *beautiful* person who was good at what he did, but it was not Tom who was going to be important, he was just smooth and good and all hollow, nothing behind the smiling white teeth and clear blue eyes. If you cracked him it would be like a china doll, nothing in the middle.

So with Bettine.

"I love you," he had protested. As far as she had known, no one had ever really loved Bettine Maunfry, though she had sold everything she had to keep people pleased and smiling at her all her life. She was not, in thinking about it, sure what she would do *if* someone loved her, or if she would know it if he did. She looked about at the magazines with the pictures of eyes and lips and the articles on how to sell one's soul.

Articles on love.

There's love and love, Anne had said.

Pleasing people. Pleasing everyone, so that they would please Bettine. Pretty children got rewards for crying and boys got spanked. While the world was pacified, it would not hurt Bettine.

Eyes and lips, primal symbols.

She made up carefully, did her hair, added the last items to her packing.

Except her handwork, which kept her sane. Click, click.
Mindless sanity, rhythms and patterns. There was light from
the window now. Probably breakfast would arrive soon, but
she was not hungry.

And finally came the noise of the doors, and the steps ascending the tower.

Richard Collier came. He shut the door behind him and
looked down at her frowning; and she stood up in front of
the only window.

Look them in the eyes, the Queen had said. She looked at
Richard that way, the Queen's way, and he evidently did not
like it.

"The name," he said.

She came to him, her eyes filling with tears in spite of herself. "I don't want to tell you," she said. "It would hurt somebody; and if you trusted me you'd let me straighten it out. I
can get your file back for you."

"You leave that to me," Richard said. "The name, girl, and
no more—"

She had no idea why she did it. Certainly Richard's ex-
pression was one of surprise, as if he had calculated something completely wrong. There was blood on her, and the
long needle buried between his ribs, and he slid down to lie
on the floor screaming and rolling about, or trying to. It was
a very soundproof room; and no one came. She stood and
watched, quite numb in that part of her which ought to have
been conscience; if anything feeling mild vindication.

"Bettine," she said quietly, and sat down and waited for
him to die and for someone who had brought him to the
tower to miss him. Whoever had the numbers was free to use
them now; there would be a new order in the city; there
would be a great number of changes. She reckoned that if she
had ordered her life better she might have been better prepared, and perhaps in a position to escape. She was not. She
had not planned. It's not the moments that can be planned,
the Roman would say; it's the lives . . . that lead to them.

And did London's life . . . lead to Bettine Maunfry? She
suspected herself of a profound thought. She was even proud
of it. Richard's eyes stared blankly now. There had not been
a great deal of pain. She had not wanted that, particularly,
although she would not have shrunk from it. In a moment,
there was not time to shrink.

There was power and there was love, and she had gotten through life with neither. She did not see what one had to do with the other; nothing, she decided, except in the sense that there really never had been a Bettine Maunfry, only a doll which responded to everyone else's impulses. And there had been nothing of her to love.

She would not unchoose what she had done; that was Elizabeth's test of happiness. She wondered if Richard would.

Probably not, when one got down to moments; but Richard had not been particularly smart in some things.

I wonder if I could have been Mayor, she thought. Somewhere I decided about that, and never knew I was deciding.

There was a noise on the stairs now. They were coming. She sat still, wondering if she shought fight them too, but decided against it. She was not, after all, insane. It was politics. It had to do with the politics of His Honor the Mayor and of one Bettine, a girl, who had decided not to give a name.

They broke in, soldiers, who discovered the Mayor's body with great consternation. They laid hands on her and shouted questions.

"I killed him," she said. They waved rifles at her, accusing her of being part of the revolution.

"I led my own," she said.

They looked very uncertain then, and talked among themselves and made calls to the city. She sat guarded by rifles, and they carried the Mayor out, poor dead Richard. They talked out the murder and wondered that she could have had the strength to drive the needle so deep. Finally—incredibly—they questioned the jailer as to what kind of prisoner she was, as if they believed that she had been more than the records showed, the imprisoned leader of some cause, the center of the movement they had been hunting. They talked about more guards. Eventually she had them, in great number, and by evening, all the Tower was ringed with soldiery, and heavy guns moved into position, great batteries of them in the inner court. Two days later she looked out the window and saw smoke where outer London was, and knew there was riot in the town.

The guards treated her with respect. Bettine Maunfry, they called her when they had to deal with her, not girl, and not Bettine. They called on her—of all things, to issue a taped call for a cease-fire.

But of her nightly companions . . . nothing. Perhaps they were shy, for at night a guard stood outside in the anteroom. Perhaps, after all, she was a little mad. She grieved for their absence, not for Richard and not for Tom, living in this limbo of tragic comedy. She watched the city burn and listened to the tread of soldiers in the court, and watched the gun crews from her single window. It was the time before supper, when they left her a little to herself—if a guard at the stairside door was privacy; they had closed off the anteroom as they usually did, preparing to deliver her dinner.

"Quite a turmoil you've created."

She turned from the window, stared at Marc in amazement. "But it's daytime."

"I *am* a little faded," he said, looking at his hand, and looked up again. "How are you, Bettine?"

"It's ridiculous, isn't it?" She gestured toward the courtyard and the guns. "They think I'm dangerous."

"But you are."

She thought about it, how frightened they were and what was going on in London. "They keep asking me for names. Today they threatened me. I'm not sure I'm *that* brave, Marc, I'm really not."

"But you don't know any."

"No," she said. "Of course I don't. So I'll be counted as brave, won't I?"

"The other side needs a martyr, and you're it, you know that."

"How does it go out there? Do the Queen's spies tell her?"

"Oh, it's violent, quite. If I were alive I'd be out there; it's a business for soldiers. The starships are hanging off just waiting. The old Mayor was dealing under the table in favoring a particular company, and the company that supported him had its offices wrecked. . . . others just standing by waiting to move in and give support to the rebels, to outmaneuver their own rivals. The ripple goes on to stars you've never seen."

"That's amazing."

"You're not frightened."

"Of course I'm frightened."

"There was a time a day ago when you might have ended up in power; a mob headed this way to get you out, but the troops got them turned."

"We'll it's probably good they didn't get to me. I'm afraid I wouldn't know what to do with London if they gave it to me. Elizabeth was right."

"But the real leaders of the revolution have come into the light now; they use your name as a cause. It's the spark they needed so long. Your name is their weapon."

She shrugged.

"They've a man inside the walls, Bettine . . . do you understand me?"

"No. I don't."

"I couldn't come before; it was still your moment . . . these last few days. None of us could interfere. It wouldn't be right. But I'm edging the mark . . . just a little. I always do. Do you understand me now, Bettine?"

"I'm going to die?"

"He's on his way. It's one of the revolutionaries . . . not the loyalists. The revolution needs a martyr; and they're afraid you *could* get out. They can't have their own movement taken away from their control by some mob. You'll die, yes. And they'll claim the soldiers killed you to stop a rescue. Either way, they win."

She looked toward the door, bit her lip. She heard a door open, heard steps ascending; a moment's scuffle.

"I'm here," Marc said.

"Don't you have to go away again? Isn't this . . . something I have to do?"

"Only if you wish."

The inner door opened. A wild-eyed man stood there, with a gun, which fired, right for her face. It *hurt*. It seemed too quick, too ill-timed; she was not ready, had not said all she wanted to say.

"There are things I wanted to do," she protested.

"There always are."

She had not known Marc was still there; the place was undefined and strange.

"Is it over? Marc, I wasn't through. I'd just figured things out."

He laughed and held out his hand. "Then you're ahead of most."

He was clear and solid to her eyes; it was the world which had hazed. She looked about her. There were voices, a busy hum of accumulated ages, time so heavy the world could scarcely bear it.

"I could have done better."

The hand stayed extended, as if it were important. She reached out hers, and his was warm.

"Till the sun dies," he said.

"Then what?" It was the first question.

He told her.

ICE

(Moscow)

Beauty was all about ancient Moskva, in the vast whiteness at world's end. Moskva lived through the final ages wrapped in snows, while forests advanced and retreated, and the ships from the stars stopped coming. The City lost contact with other cities, caring little, for its struggle was its own, and peculiar to itself, a struggle of the soul, an inward and endless war which each citizen fought in his or her own way. In that struggle Moskva became as it was, a city no longer stone, not in its greater part, but wood, which it had been at its beginning. Ah, ancient, ancient monuments lay beneath, frozen, warped and changed, serving as mere foundations. Here and there throughout the city vast heads of statues and the tops of ancient buildings still thrust up at strange angles, but the features and the corners were blurred, scoured white and round and clean by the winds, stones become one with the snows, as the snows had lapped all the past in purest white and blurred all past and all to come.

But the present buildings, gaily colored, carved, embellished, the warmhearted buildings in which the people lived, were made of wood from the last and retreating forest, wood on which the people had shown their last and highest artistry. On every inch of the surfaces and columns, flowers twined, human faces stared out, vines and designs of bright colors entangled the gaze. Skins of animals adorned the floors, and bunches of dried flowers, memories of brief summer, sat on tables which were likewise carved and painted red and green and gold and blue. Hearths in every home burned bright, sending up cheery dark smoke which the winds carried away as soon as it touched the sky.

The people walked the snowy streets done up in furs edged

with bright felt embroideries, reds and blues and greens, with border patterns in the most intricate stitchery, lilies and flowers and golden ears of grain; with scarves hand-stitched in convolute vine patterns, all jewel-bright, each garment a glory, a memory of color, a delight to the eye. All the soul of the people who lived in Moskva was poured into the making of this polychrome beauty, all the rich heritage of the lands and the fields and the passion of their hearts, both into the wooden buildings within Moskva's wooden walls, and into the gay colors they wore. There were dances, celebrations of life . . . dancing and singing, from which the participants fell down exhausted and full of warmth and joy, celebrations in which they danced life itself, to the bright whirling of cloth and tassels and scarves and the stamp of broidered boots, all picked out with flowers and reindeer and horses. Music of strings and music of voices rose from Moskva into the winds.

But above the city the songs changed, and the voice of the winds overpowered them, changing the brave words into wailing, and the wailing at last into a whisper of snow powdering along the rough ice of Moskva's interior skein of rivers, which were thawed only for a few weeks a year, and most times were frozen deep and solid . . . grains hissed along icy ridges outside the walls, and whispered of the north, of ground endlessly covered with snow, pure of any foot's imprint, forever.

White . . . but seldom truly white . . . was the world outside the wooden walls. Above it, the sun died its slow eonslong death, in glorious flarings of radiations which brought nightly curtains of moving light across the skies; it brought days of strange color, apricot and lavenders and oranges and eerie minglings of subtler shades, which touched the snows and the ice and streamed across them with glories and flares that made a thousand delicate shades of light and shadowings. The snows knew many subtleties—nights when the opal moon hung frighteningly low, in a sky sometimes violet and sometimes approaching blue, and very rarely black and dusted with ancient stars. At such times the snows went bright and pale and so, so still, with the black bristling shades of pines southward and the endless stillness of snow northward. Or starker pallor, storm . . . when the clouds went gray and strange and the wind took on an eerie voice, and the snow began to fly, for days and days of white as if the world had stopped being, and there was only white and wind.

This was the struggle, the reason of the bright fires, the bright colors, the noisy celebrations, the images of flowers and vines. Other cities round about might already have perished. No travelers came. But the soul of Moskva held firm, and their busyness about their own affairs saved them, because they refused to look up, or out, and their bright colors held against the snows, and their rough, man-made beauty prevailed against the terrible shifting beauty of the ice.

Bravest of all in Moskva were those who *could* venture outside the walls, who wrapped themselves in their bright furs and their courage and ventured out into the frozen wastes— the hunters, the loggers, the farers-forth, who could look out into the cold whiteness and keep the colors in their hearts.

But even to them sometimes the sickness came, which began to fade them, and which set their eyes to staring out into the horizons; for once that coldness did come on them, their lives were not long. There were wolves outside the walls, there were dire dangers, and deaths waiting always, but the white death was inward and quiet and direst of all.

Andrei Gorodin had no fear in him. Winter did not daunt him, and when the snows came and the foxes and ermines turned their coats to snowiest white, he was one of the rare ones who continued to go out, he and his piebald pony, a shaggy beast as gay in its coat as the city with its painting, looking out on the icy world through a shag of yellow mane and forelock that let all the world wonder whether there was a horse within it. Like Andrei, the pony had no fear, immune to the terrors which seized on other beasts allied to man, terrors which turned their ribs gaunt and their eyes stark, so that eventually they fell to pining and died. Not Umnik, who jogged along the snows surefooted and regarding the world with a seldom-seen and mistrustful eye.

His master, Andrei Vasilyevitch Gorodin, returning home after a day's good hunt, rode wrapped in lynx fur, with belts and boots of bright embroidered leather; and about his face a flowered leather scarf, which Anna Ivanovna had made for him (who made him other fine, bright gifts, storing them up in a carven chest beneath her bed . . . she was his bride-to-be this spring, when spring should come, when weddings were lucky). A brace of fat hares hung frozen from his saddle. His bow, from which gay tassels fluttered, hung at his back; and from his traps he had a snow fox which he planned to give Anna to make her an edging for a cape. He whistled as he rode, with Umnik's breath puffing merrily on the still air, with the crunch of hooves on crusted snow and the creak of the harness to keep the time. He had a flask with him, and from time to time he drank lightly from it, warming his belly. About him the snow gleamed pure white, for clouds veiled the sun, and he had no present need of the carved eyeshields which hung about his neck, and which, worn with the flower-broidered scarf, made him look like some strange bright-patterned beast atop a piebald shaggy one. It was one of the rare calm days, so quiet that he and Umnik seemed alone in the world; and when he stopped the pony to rest, savoring the quiet air, he could hear the crack of ice in the cold, and the fall of a branchload of snow in the lightest breath of air. He listened to such sounds, and just a slight touch of the silence came into his heart, which was dangerous. He gathered his courage and whistled to the pony, urged him on. He began to sing, louder and louder in the vast silence of the white world, and Umnik moved along right merrily, flicking his ears to the song.

But the song did not last, and the silence returned, seeming to muffle even the crunch of ice under Umnik's hooves. And all at once Umnik stopped, and his head turned to the north: his ears pricked up and his nostrils strained to drink the air. The pony began to tremble then, and Andrei quickly slid his bow from off his shoulder and strung it, and took a red-fletched arrow from his broidered quiver, then looked about, north, at the white vastness and its gentle rolls, south at the edge of pine forest beside which they rode. The pony looked fixedly toward a narrow view of the open land beyond two hills. He stood rigid, his mane lifting in a little cold wind, gathering crystals of blowing snow in its coarse yellow hairs.

There was nothing. Andrei tapped Umnik with his heels. Sometimes horses saw ghosts, so the old hunters said, and then the wasting began, and they would die, but this was not like Umnik, a plain-minded beast, not given to fancies. Umnik moved forward feather-footed and skittish. Andrei believed the horse, which had never yet played him false, and he kept his bow in hand and an arrow on the string, his eyes toward the north, as the horse gazed while it moved, though its course was westerly and homeward.

For a moment the gray clouds parted and the sun shone through, gilding the drifts with flaring colors. Umnik sidestepped and shied, throwing his head. A white shape was in

the glare, slow and slinking . . . a wolf, white as a winter
wind. Andrei's heart clenched; and he raised and bent his
bow, between fear of it and desire for its beauty, for he had
never seen such a beast. The arrow sped as horse and wolf
moved, and the wolf was gone, over the rim of a drift. He
clapped heels to Umnik's sides, once and again, and the brave
pony went through the drift and off the way, reluctantly and
warily. The clouds had closed again, the sun was gone, and a
sudden gust of wind whipped off the snows of the right-hand
hill, carrying stinging particles into his eyes.

Umnik shied, and Andrei reined him around, patted the
pony's shaggy neck and rode him back again. There was
nothing, not wolf or so much as a footprint or the tiny
wound of an arrow's feathers in the snowbanks. He cast
about for the arrow, trampling the whole area with Umnik's
hooves, for it was a well-made shaft and he was not pleased
to lose it, or to be so puzzled. He thought perhaps it had
gone into a deep drift, and surely it had, for try as he would
he could not turn it up. He gave up finally, turned the pony
about and set him on his way, trying to pretend that nothing
had happened—the sun was always deceptive, and he had
looked with eyes unshielded, never wise; he might have
dreamed the wolf. But the arrow itself was gone. As he rode,
the world seemed colder, the snow starker white, and now,
like the piebald pony, he longed for the city and the bright
and busy streets of human measure. He rode along with the
frozen carcasses of his hunt dangling at his knee, now and
again looking over his shoulder to mark how the east was
darkening. He wished he had not delayed so long for the arrow, nor trifled with wolves, because it was a long ride yet.

He tried again to whistle, but his lips were dry, and the
noise Umnik made in moving seemed muffled and not as
loud as it ought. The wind gusted violently at his back.

Snow began to fall, when never in the morning had it
looked as if it could, so white the clouds had been; but the
day had gotten fouler and fouler since he had delayed, and
now he began to be much concerned. The wind blew, sighing,
whistling, picking up the snow it had just laid down as well,
to drive it in fine streams along the crusted surface and off
the crests of frozen drifts. Umnik knew the hazard; the little
horse kept moving steadily, but he threw his head as the wind
seemed to acquire voices, and those voices seemed to howl on
this side and on that of them.

"Go," Andrei asked of the pony, "go, my clever one, haste, haste," for the wind came now harder at their backs, a wind with many voices, like the voices of wolves. But the pony kept his head, saving his strength. Umnik passed the last hill, then, halfway down the downward slope, began to run with all his might, the homeward stretch which should, round the hill and beyond, bring them to the city wall. Howls behind them now were unmistakable, coming off the hillside on the left. Umnik cleared the hillside at an all-out pace, with Moskva now in sight, and Andrei lifted up the horn which hung at his belt and blew it now with all that was in him, a sound all but lost in the wind; again and again he blew . . . and to his joy the great wooden gates of Moskva began to open for him in the white veil of snow.

Umnik's flying hooves thundered over the icy bridge, up to the gates and through, over new snow at the gateway and onto the trampled streets of the city; the doors swung shut. Andrei reined in, circled Umnik as he put on a brave face, waved a jaunty salute at old Pyotr and son Fedor who kept the gates. Then he trotted Umnik on into the narrow streets, past citizens bundled against the falling snow, folk who knew him, bright-cheeked children who looked up in delight and waved at a hunter's passing.

He turned in toward the cozy house of Ivan Nikolaev, two houses, in truth, which, neighbors, had leaned together for warmth and companionship years ago and finally grown together the year his own parents died, leaving him to the Nikolaevs and their kin. The carven-fenced yards had become one, the houses joined, and so did the painted stables where the Nikolaevs' bay pony and the Orlovs' three goats waited, Umnik's stay-at-home stablemates.

The household had been waiting for him; the side door opened, and Katya his foster mother came out bundled against the cold, to take Umnik's reins. He dropped to the snowy yard and tugged down the scarf to kiss her brow and hug her a welcome, cheerfully then slung the frozen game over his shoulder while he stripped off the pony's harness to carry it indoors. Umnik shook himself thoroughly and trotted away on his own to the grain and the warm stall waiting, and Andrei, slinging the saddle to his shoulder with one hand and hugging mother Katya with the other arm, headed for the porch. She would have worried for him, with the hour late and the snow beginning; she was all smiles now. And with a second slam of the door Anna was coming out too, her cheeks burned red by the wind, her eyes bright. She came running to him, her fair braids flying bare, her embroidered coat and skirts turned pale in the blowing snow; he dropped the gear and clapped her in his arms and swung her about as he had done when they were children of the same year; he kissed her (lightly, for her mother stood by laughing) then dragged the harness up again and walked with his arm about her and Katya along beside, lifted his hand from Anna's shoulder to wave at her brother Ilya, who had come outside still bundling up.

The oldest Nikolaev was a woodcutter, and his son Ivan a woodcutter; but young Ilya, Anna's twin, of no stout frame, was an artist, a carver, whose work was all about them, the bright posts of the porch, the flowered shutters . . . "Ah," Ilya said to him cheerfully, "back safe—what else could he be? I told her so." He hugged Ilya a snowy welcome too, stamped his boots clean and hung the game on the porch, then whisked inside with all the rest, into warmth like a wall. He hung the bow and harness in the inner porch, stripped off snowy furs and changed to his indoor boots. Katya bustled off and brought him back tepid water to drink, and mistress Orlov met them all at the inside door with hot tea. There was the smell of the women's delightsome cooking, and the cheer of the mingled families who beamed and gave him welcome as he came into the common room, a babble of children inevitable and inescapable in the house. Young Ivan came running to be picked up and flung about, and Andrei lifted him gladly, tired as he was. Fire crackled in the hearth and they all were gathered, settled finally for a meal, himself . . . a Gorodin; and Nikolaevs and Orlovs young and old, with the warm air smelling as the house always smelled, of wood chips and resins and leathers and furs and good cooking.

Then the fear seemed very far away.

He rested, with a full belly, and they drank steaming tea and a little vodka. Old Nikolaev and son Ivan talked their craft, where they should cut in the spring to come; and grandfather Orlov and his son, carpenters, talked of the porch they were going to repair down the street on the city hall. Grandmother Orlov sat in her chair which was always near the fire, tucked up with flowered pillows and quilts; the

children—there were seven, among the prolific Orlovs—
played by the warm hearth; and the women talked and
stitched and invented patterns. "Tell stories," the children
begged of any who would; drink passed about again, and it
was that pleasant hour. The young would begin the tale-tell-
ing, and the elders would finish, for they had always seen
deeper snows and stranger sights and colder winters.

"Tell us," little Ivan asked, bouncing against Andrei's knee,
"ah, tell us about the hunt today." Andrei sighed, taking his
arm from about Anna's waist, and smiled at the round little
face and bounced Ivan on his foot, holding two small hands,
joked with him, and drew squeals. He told the tale with flair
and flourish, warmed to the telling while the children settled
in a half-ring about his feet; his friend Ilya picked up a fresh
block of pine and his favorite knife, a blade very fine and
keen. . . . Most of all Anna listened, looked up at him when
he looked down, her eyes very bright and soft. The wind still
howled outside, but they were all warmed by each other,
while the timbers cracked and boomed now and again with
the cold. He told of the wild ride home, of the wolves . . .
wolves, for something in him flinched at telling of the Wolf,
and of the lost arrow. Little Ivan's eyes grew round as buttons, and when he came to the part about the closed gate,
and how it had opened, the children all clapped their hands
but Ivan, who sat with his eyes still round and his mouth
wide agape.

"For shame," said his grandmother, sweeping the child
against her quilt-wrapped knees. "You've frightened him, Andrei."

"I'm not afraid," the child exclaimed, and shrugged free to
mime a bowshot. "I shall grow up and be a hunter outside the
walls, like Andrei."

"What, not a carpenter?" his grandfather asked.

"No, I shall be *brave,*" the little boy said, and there was a
sudden silence in the room, a hurt, a loneliness that Andrei
felt to the heart—alone of Gorodins, of hunters in this house,
and a guest, living on parents' ancient friendship. He had
never meant to steal a son's heart away. Then a timber
cracked quite loudly, and the roof shed a few icicles and everyone laughed at the silence, to drive it away.

"That you shall be," said Ilya, and reached to ruffle the
little boy's hair. "Braver than I. I shall make you a wolf, how
will you like that?"

The child's eyes danced, and quickly he deserted to Ilya's knee, and hung there watching Ilya's deft blade peel fragrant curls from the pine—Ilya, who was Anna's very likeness, woman-beautiful, whose delicate hands likewise had no aptitude for his father's work, but who made beauty in wood, most skilled in all Moskva. Andrei watched as the child did, and with amazing swiftness the wood took on a wolf's dire shape. "I remember wolves," grandfather Orlov began, and childish eyes diverted again, traveled back and forth from Ilya's fingers to the old man's face, delightfully frightened.

Andrei held Anna's hand, and drew her against him, a bundle of furs and skirts beside the crackling fire. He listened to this tale he had heard before, and grandfather Orlov's voice seemed far from him; even Anna, against his side, seemed distant from him. He watched Ilya's razor-edged blade winking in the firelight and more and more surely saw the wolf emerge from the wood. He heard the snow fall; he had never truly *heard* it before: it needed silence, and the sense of the night outside, as the flakes settled thicker and thicker like goose down upon the roof, and their voices went up against the wind and fled away into the cold.

They spoke each of wolves that evening, and he did not hear with all his heart, nor even shiver now. He watched at last as the stories ended, and Ilya handed the wolf to the boy Ivan, with all the children crowded jealously about, a clamor swiftly dismissed for bed, blanket-heaped cots in the farthest room of the loft, and deep down mattresses and coziness and the rush of the wind at the shutters.

"Good night," he bade mother Katya and father Ivan, and "Good night," he kissed Anna. Then he and Ilya sought their room in the loft as well, bedded down together as they had slept since they were boys like Ivan, snugged down in piles of quilts and a deep down mattress.

"I was afraid," he confessed to Ilya when they had been some time settled, side by side in the dark. "I should have told the boy."

"Boys grow up," Ilya said. "And boys grow wiser. Do not we all?"

He thought of that, and lay there awake, staring at the beams and listening, hearing the wind above them, very close. It seemed to him that the down beneath him was like the snowdrifts, endlessly deep and soft; and if he shut his eyes he could see the blue darkness of the night and a ghost-white form which loped over the snows, with beauty in its running. Deep soft drifts, and lupine eyes full of night . . . a triangular face and blowing snow, and wolf-eyes holding secrets—a shape which coursed the winds, drifts which became other wolves, snow-cold and coursing down upon his hapless dreams like hunters upon prey.

Then he was afraid with a deep fear, remembering the arrow, for the foremost wolf bore a wound which dropped blood from its heart, and the droplets became ruby ice, which fell without a sound.

He woke the next morning in an inner silence deeper than the day before, though the timbers groaned, and snow had slid upon the roof, tumbling down the eaves, and this had wakened him and Ilya. "No hunting this day," said Ilya, hearing the wind. He said nothing, but listened to the storm.

And as the children wakened and shivered downstairs, and the women stirred about, and there was no more lying abed, Ilya stirred out, quickly pulling his boots on, and so did Andrei, hearing the great town bell ringing, muted and soft in the storm which lapped the morning.

He and Ilya and Anna and the other Nikolaevs and Orlovs with strength to help dressed in their warmest clothing and ventured out into a town gone white. Drifts lay man-high in the streets; they hitched up the ponies, and worked . . . like ghosts, moving through the pale driving snow; worked until backs ached, cleared paths, braced roofs, braced the wall itself. The market opened, very quickly empty, and the winds kept a fury which sang through the air, and carried the snow back as swiftly as they could move it. They surrendered at last and returned to their homes, to warm meals and warm fires and patient cheer.

But within the house the silence gained yet a deeper hold, as snow piled about the walls and the windsong grew more distant. It was that manner of storm which could set in and last for days; in which the white loneliness settled close about the town. Andrei tied a rope about himself and went out in the last of day, fearing for Umník's safety and that of the other beasts; but he found them well, snug in their stable and warm with the snow about. He started back again, into the white drifts, following the rope which he had tied about him, which vanished into white. Not even the shadow of the house was visible in the storm; and when he looked back, he could not see the stable.

White. All was white. He looked all about, suddenly dreading the slinking form that might be within that whiteness, itself immaculate and swift as the northwind. He imagined that he might see suddenly two strange darknesses staring at him, wolfish slanted; pink lolling tongue, and white, white teeth.

He looked behind him, turning with a start. With haste he seized hard upon the rope and followed it, pushed through a wall of blowing snow, stumbled against the buried porch and climbed to the door, found it frozen shut. His nape prickled, and he would not look back. Something breathed there, in the silence of the howling wind, and he would not turn to see. He rapped at the door, called those inside, refusing panic. But the silence grew, and he could hardly move from the chill in his bones when the door opened and Anna and Ilya snatched him inside.

"Oh, he is cold," Anna said, and they hastened him to the fire in the inmost hall, sitting him there to strip off his furs; they heated blankets before the fire and wrapped him in them, then brought him tea. All the house gathered, murmuring at some vast distance, and the children came and touched his cold hands, as did Anna and Ilya's mother, who hugged him and chafed his fingers and kissed his brow, greatly concerned. But from the mantle above the fire Ilya's wolf stared back at him.

They danced that night, and drank and sang; he drank much and laughed and yet—the silence was there.

He lay in bed that night and dreamed of blue nights and still snows, and that white shape which ran with the wind, amid moon-twinkling snowflakes and over drifts, never leaving a mark upon them.

The next day dawned clear and bright.

The whole of Moskva seemed to smile in the day, colored eaves peeking out from the deep drifts which lay between the houses, children and elders bundled like thick-limbed and thickly mittened dolls out breaking through the drifts to walk the streets and visit kin and friends. The Orlov children squealed with delight, breaking up the drifts to the stables, and breaking icicles off the eaves of the porch. Some children had sleds out on the streets, and the children clamored for their own.

But Andrei met the morning with less cheer, quietly put on his outdoor boots and his warm furs, took his gear out and saddled Umnik, who was restive and full of argument. He said no word to Anna or her parents, none to Ilya, only smiled bleakly at the children who grew quieter looking at him, and, stopping their sledding, stood like a row of huddled birds by the fence as he rode through the gate and passed down the street.

"Good morning," the neighbors said cheerfully, pausing in their snow-shoveling. "A good morning to you, Andrei Vasil-yevitch." He nodded absently and kept going. "Good morning," said white-bearded Pyotr by the gatehouse, and he forgot to return the greeting, but got down off Umnik and helped the gate wardens heave the gates inward, got up again on Umnik's back. The pony tossed his shaggy head and advanced on the drift which barred their way, lurched through it and onto smoother going, toward the bridge and the open land, snuffing the cold crisp air with red-veined nostrils and pricking up his ears as he thumped across the bridge and jogged toward the hills.

The sun climbed higher still, until it passed noon. Andrei wrapped his scarf about his face to warm his breath, and omitted the eyeshields, for there was still haze in the heavens, and the snow lay white and thick everywhere. There were few tracks, no promise of good hunting; the snow had not been long enough to turn the beasts desperate and reckless . . . nor was the day warm enough to tempt them out of hiding. He should have waited a day, but the thought of the dark loft and sitting before the fire with nothing to do oppressed him. In idleness he had evil memory for company. He came out to deny it, to laugh at it, to hunt and to win this time.

He was afraid. He had never felt the like before. Even in the bright, clear daylight he felt what he had felt in that ride to the gates, with the wolves baying at his back. He was afraid of fear . . . for the hunt was his livelihood, and when he feared too much, he could not come outside the walls.

He rose in his stirrups and looked back, settled forward again as he rode. They were long out of sight of the city's wooden walls; snowy hills and snowy fields stretched in all directions but the south, where forest stood thickly whited and iced. There was no sound but Umnik's regular moving, the creak of harness, and the whuff of breath.

Umnik moved more slowly now, having run out his first wind, wading almost knee-deep along the trail. And there was such beauty in the white snow that his fear grew less. He stopped the horse and turned and looked all about him, heard a rapid, doggish panting at his back.

He spun, hauling at the reins, and Umnik shied in the deep drift, rose on hind legs, almost falling.

Nothing was there. He steadied the horse and patted it, and nothing was there. The light grew; the clouds parted. He reached for the eyeshields as the snows gathered the sunflares, misted gold and rose and amber; Umnik stood still, and Andrei stopped with the eyeshields in his hand . . . feeling a fascination for that light—for light had concealed the Wolf. He looked to the far hills—and to the sky, into the sun. He had never looked up in his life, save a furtive glance to know the condition of the sky—but not to see it. It smote his heart. And he looked north. The wolf was there, standing watchfully on the surface of a new drift, and its eyes were like the sun, and its coat was touched with the subtle shifting colors.

He whipped Umnik and rode; he never remembered beginning . . . but he and Umnik skimmed the snows in terror, the white wolf never far.

At last the city was before them, and he took the horn from his side to blow, but the sound of it seemed dim. Umnik faltered, and he whipped the pony, drove him, up to the approach to the city, across the wooden bridge and to the southern gate, while white shapes leaped and plunged about him and voices howled, far and still, as if his hearing were dulled, and all the world was wrapped in cold. Umnik slowed as they came to the opening gates, but he whipped the pony harder, and rode upon the streets, hooves skidding on the snow, and startled citizens and children with a sled scurried from the horse's path. He stopped, looked about, and the gates were closing slowly. "The wolves," he cried, but Pyotr the gate warden looked strangely at him, continuing to heave at the gates.

Nothing had been there. The wolves were in his own eyes. He knew this suddenly, and the cold grew deeper in his heart.

"Are you all right, Andrei?" Pyotr asked.

He nodded, cold and shamed by the death he saw for himself. He reached vaguely for Umnik's reins, remembered how he had beaten the pony, and patted his neck as he led Umnik away down the street. Umnik shook himself, walked slowly and with head hanging, as if perhaps a bit of the coldness had come into his heart too, as if it had been driven there with blows.

He did not go home. He went to the house of old Mischa the hunter, which huddled small and antlered and not so bright as others between the market stalls and the public baths. Snow had drifted heavily there, almost buried it to the eaves on one side. The stone head of a forgotten hero loomed up, peering out of the snow with only the dimmest impression of features. He walked upon the porch and tied Umnik to its rail, stamped his boots and opened the first door, walked across the inner porch and rapped at the second.

There was no answer, no forbidding. "Mischa," he called, "it's Andrei Gorodin." He walked in, sweltering already in the warmth within, redolent with the smell of boiling oils and burned grease and dried herbs that was Mischa's house; antlers were everywhere, and feathers and a clutter of oddments. And a huddle of blankets before the fire . . . that was Mischa himself, a wrinkled face and dark narrow eyes and a skein of grisled hair trailing from his hood. One hand held a bundle of herbs which he had been crumbling into a saucer; there was no left hand: a wolf had gotten that, when Mischa had been a hunter himself . . . but that was before Andrei had been born. Andrei crouched down and met Mischa's sightless eyes.

"So?" asked Mischa.

The question stopped behind his lips. And slowly Mischa's hand lifted, touched his face spiderwise, drifted to his chest as if it searched for something there as well.

"A visit with no questions, Andrei Vasilyevitch?"

"I have lost my luck, Mischa."

"So." Mischa dipped up water from the kettle, ladled it into the bowl, passed it to him. He took the bowl in gloved hands, inhaled the vapor, sipped the surface, for there was danger in heat so intense after the cold outside. He drank more after a moment, but the cold did not leave, nor the veil on the world diminish.

"I see wolves," Andrei said.

The darkened eyes rested on his, wrinkle-girt as though they were set in cracked stone.

"A white wolf," Andrei said. "Snow white. Ice white."

Old Mischa crumbled more herbs into yet another bowl, ladled in more water, drank, black eyes hooded.

"I shot at it," Andrei said. "But it was there again today. I've looked into the sun, Mischa."

Mischa stared at him as if the eyes could see.

"What shall I *do,* old hunter?"

Mischa moved his left hand, showing the stump. "Appease it," he said. "That is all you can hope to do."

Andrei set down the bowl, wrapped his furred arms the tighter about him, gazed at the old hunter. Wizard. Seer of visions . . . who had had the white sickness—and lived.

"You have looked," the seer said. "You have talked to the wind and heard it answer; you have run ahead of the wolf. And the light has got into your eyes, as it did your father's, my old friend. It took all of him. I gave it part of me. And I am still alive, Andrei Vasilyevitch. Your mother birthed you and pined away; and so they both went. But I am still alive, friend's son."

Andrei stumbled up and hurried for the door, looked back at the wizened face shrouded in gray hood, single hand cupping the bowl. He felt the cold even greater than before, on face and in heart, wherever the blind hunter's fingers had touched. "I will bring your fee," he said, "on my next hunt, a fat rabbit or two, Mischa."

"I take nothing," the old man said. "Not from you, until you see, Andrei Vasilyevitch."

He fled the house, stamped outside and closed the outer door. Umnik waited. He walked down the step to the pony, and noticed for the first time how the paint was peeling on the house opposite, how all the colors of Moskva looked gaudy, how stained the snow and how disarrayed the people, bundled in mismatched furs.

Slowly, with a squinting of his eye and a turning of his shoulder, he looked *up.* Colors shifted in the sky, danced along the rooftops, ran the ridges, streaming glories of pink and gold. *This* was beauty. About him was painted ugliness.

All his heart longed to go on looking, to go out to the ice and ride into the north, into the pure fair beauty.

But the Wolf was there. And the beauty killed.

He shuddered, took Umnik's reins and walked slowly into the street, walked down it among people who stared curiously and whispered behind their hands. This was the wasting. He knew now . . . what drank up the souls of those who took ill with the sickness. It was vision. It was looking on all that hands made and knowing that one had only to look up—and

having looked, to yield to that blankness which would exist
after all the world was done. To measure one's self and one's
acts against that white sheet, and to find them small, and unlovely after all.

Beauty waited, outside the walls, near as a look at the un-
guarded sky; beauty waited . . . and the Wolf did.

Appease it, the old hunter said, no longer a hunter, Mischa
who saw no more sunrises, who had given a part of himself
to the wolves . . . to the Wolf.

He went home. Ilya and Ivan Nikolaev ran outside to meet
him, and the women and children too, concerned for him.
Anna came, and Katya, each hugging him. Quietly he took
the harness from Umnik and expected he should go away to
his stable . . . but Umnik stood. "Take him," he bade little
Ivan, and the boy led the pony away. Andrei looked after the
plodding horse and shivered. He felt within his gloved hand
another hand, felt a touch upon his arm. . . . He looked into
Anna's loving eyes, into her face, saw flaws which he had
never seen before, the length of nose, the breadth of cheek,
the imperfection of her brow. On it was the tiny fleck of a
scar, not centered, and her hair, which he had always thought
bright as the sunset on snow, was dull, the braids lusterless
against the snowflakes blowing upon them, tiny stars sticking
in the loose hair. . . . This was beauty, recalling cold, and
fear.

"Come in," Anna urged him, and he surrendered the
harness to Ilya, walked with Anna's hand in his, before them
all to the house and the inner porch. He shed his outdoor
boots and furs, and greeted the children indoors with a touch
of his hand and greeted the old ones by the hearth with a
kiss, seeing everywhere mortality, man's short span, and
smallness.

"Andrei?" Anna sat by him, near the fireside, taking his
hand again. He kissed and held hers because it was kind, but
love and hope were dried up in him . . . a hunter who could
not go outside the walls again, who sat with his soul withering
within him.

There was nothing beautiful among men. There was only
that beauty above and about Moskva. It would draw the
mind from him, or cost the light of his eyes. He stared into
the fire, and it was nothing to the brilliance of the sun on ice.

A silence settled about him, whether it was the silence of
the house, that they knew there was something amiss with

him, or the silence in his soul. He thought how easy it should
be, how direly easy tomorrow noon, to walk outside, to stare
at the sun until he had no more sight, but even then, there
would be the memory.

He thought again and again of old Mischa, who had lost
his eyes and lost his hand . . . appease it: but which had
gone first, which availed against the Wolf? He should have
asked.

"Andrei?" Ilya took his arm. He heard someone weeping
by him, perhaps Anna, or some other one who loved him.
Perhaps it was himself. He saw Ilya's face before his, much
concerned, saw a hand pass before his eyes, heard them all
discussing his plight, but he could not come back from that
far place and argue with them. He had no desire in him.

They fed him, set food into his hands; and he ate, hardly
tasting it. At last Anna took his face between her soft hands
and kissed him on the brow; as mother Katya did. "What is
wrong with Andrei?" a child's voice asked. He would have
explained to the child but someone else did: "He is ill. He is
hurt. Go to bed, child."

"His hands are cold," said another; and Anna's voice:
"Lock the doors. Oh, lock the doors, don't let him stray."
Some did walk away to die, taken with the wasting, who
sought the night, and frozen death.

"I shall not go," he said, great effort to speak; and no
easier when he had done it. It cheered them all. They hugged
him and chafed his hands.

"Perhaps," said Anna's still, faraway voice, "he only
looked up a little moment. Perhaps he will get well."

"He will," someone vowed, but he was not sure who.
Easier to retreat, back into that far place, but they gave him
no peace.

"I will see him to bed," Ilya said. "Go, sleep. I will take
care of him. No, Anna—Anna, please go."

Someone kissed him, gently, sadly. The house fell then
slowly into silence. He rested, staring at the fire, disturbed
only when Ilya would reach to stir the embers. "Will you go
upstairs?" Ilya asked at last. "Dare you sleep?"

He roused himself out of kindness to them who loved him,
rose, and rising, caught at the mantlepiece, stared fixedly at
the face of Ilya's carven wolf, which seemed starker and
truer than all else in the room. He looked at the other work
which Ilya had made, the carven mantle itself, ran his fingers

over the writhing wooden vines and leaves, touched the carven flowers, traced the gaudy, garish colors.

"I have seen beauty," he said. "Ilya, you do not know. It waits out there—"

"Andrei," Ilya said.

"I have seen colors . . . you have never seen."

Ilya reached out and turned his face toward him, lightly slapped his cheek. There was a terrible pain in Ilya's face, like Anna's pain.

"Tell me," Ilya said.

He thought of it, and would not.

"Andrei, if you go, Anna will follow. Do you understand? Anna loves you; and you will never go alone."

He thought of this too, and deep within, tainted by self and small, there was a kindness where love had been, that was the other pole which drew him. The death outside pulled at him, but within the walls there was a bond to living souls, so that at last he knew what he ought to choose, which was Mischa's way. He would not wish this torment on those who loved him. Not on Anna.

"Is there still sun?" he asked.

"No," Ilya said softly. "The sun has gone."

"Tomorrow then."

"What, tomorrow?" Ilya asked. "What will be tomorrow?"

It was hard to resist Ilya, close to him—so long his friend. Brother. Other self. "There was a wolf," he said slowly, leaning there against the mantel, and fingering the carvings Ilya's hand had made. "I hunted it . . . and it hunts me. I have talked with old Mischa, do you know, Ilya? And Mischa knows that beast. Mischa said I must appease it, and then I shall be free; and so I shall. You love beauty, Ilya, and I hunted it, and I have seen it . . . out there, I have seen the sun, and the light, and the ice, and I am cold, Ilya. I shall look now by little stolen moments and sooner or later I will have to go outside the walls. Then it will be waiting there."

"Anna—would follow you. Do you understand that, Andrei? How much she loves you?"

He nodded. "So," he said, still staring at the wolf, "so I shall not wish to go. I shall try not to, Ilya."

"What . . . did you see?"

He looked into Ilya's eyes, and saw there a touch of that same cold. Of furtive desire. "No," he said. "Let be. Don't stay near me. Let me be."

"So that you can go, and die?"

He shrugged. Ilya stared at him, distraught. He patted Ilya's shoulder, walked away to the ladder to the loft. Stopped, for he could hear the wind outside, calling him, to the wolf. "It's there," he said. "Just outside."

"I shall watch you," Ilya said. "I shall; Anna will, one and then the other of us. We will not let you go."

He looked toward the door, seeing beyond it, into the blue night. Ilya took his arm, had a burning candle with him, to light them to the loft. "Come," Ilya bade him, and he climbed the wooden ladder that was carved with flowers, up among the painted columns and posts of the loft, quietly passed the roomful of sleeping children. There was their own nook; Ilya shut the door, touched the candle to the night lamp and blew the wick out, small ordinary acts, done every night of their lives, comforting now. Andrei moved of life-long habit, undid his belt and hung it on the bedpost on his side, took off his boots, crawled beneath the cold, heavy bed-clothes. Ilya tucked him in when he had lain down, as once Katya had nightly climbed the stairs to do; and he feigned quick sleep. Ilya stood there a moment, walked around then with a creaking of the aged boards, climbed in the other side.

The bed was like ice; it remained so, but Andrei did not shiver. He lay still, and listened to the wind, listened to foot-steps around the door downstairs, soft, padding steps that would never print the snow. Listened to the blowing of flakes from off the rooftree, and the fall of those particles onto drifts. Timbers boomed, like lightning strikes, and he would jump, and lie still again.

At last he could resist it no more, and stirred, thrust a foot for the cold air and the floor. "Andrei," Ilya said at once, turned, rose on an elbow, reached out to take his shoulder. "Are you all right, Andrei?"

He lay back. "Let me go," he said finally. "Ilya, the wolf is out there. It will always be."

"Hush, be still." And when he moved, hardly aware that he moved to rise, Ilya held him back. "It waits," he said, pro-testing. "It waits, Ilya, and the cold will spread, more than to me alone. You know that."

"Hush." Ilya quietly rolled from the bed, and went around to his side, sat down there. "I shall get no sleep," Ilya said. "I shall never know if you are not walking in yours. How shall I rest, Andrei? I promised Anna I would watch you."

He did not want to listen to this, but it touched through the numbness that possessed him. "You should let me go," he said. "I shall go . . . tomorrow or the next day. It will never be far, just outside the door. Umnik and me—it will have us."

"Hush." Ilya wrapped his wrist in his belt, then attached it to the bedpost; this he allowed, because it was Ilya, and he knew how greatly Ilya grieved; it was not fair that Ilya should worry so. Ilya took great pains, with this and with the other one, sat there, straightened his hair, his hand very gentle. "Sleep now," Ilya said. "Go to sleep; you will not wander in your dreams. You are safe."

He shut his eyes, thinking that the day would come, and other nights, and when he shut his eyes, the wolf was there, no less than he had been before, eyes like the sun, a white wolf in blue night, invisible against the snow which lay thick in the yard. The horses whickered softly, disturbed. Goats bleated . . . no need of alarm for them. They were safe in their warm stable, where the cold would never come . . . and it was the cold which waited.

He felt Ilya draw back, heard the creak of boards, the door open, heard Ilya go down the ladder. He felt a little distress then and pulled to be free, but Ilya's knots were snug, and the vision drank him back again, the blue night, the pale snows. Somewhere he heard the softest of sounds, and he dreamed the wolf retreated, standing warily out by the fence. And others were there, white and gaunt with famine. A vision came to him, of the house door opening softly in the dark and a figure in his furs, who carried his bow and his shafts. Umnik nickered softly, came out from the stable on his own, and his ears were pricked up and his eyes were full of the moving curtains of light which leapt and danced and flowed across the blue heavens. . . . The aurora, uncommonly bright and strange. The horse walked forward, nuzzled an offered hand and the two of them stood together, man and pony, beneath the glory of the sky. Slowly the man looked up, his face to the light, and it was Ilya, whose eyes, angry, showed the least fatal quickness as they gazed at the heavens . . . curiosity, and openness,

"There," Ilya said, tugging at Umnik's long mane, whispering and stretching out the bow like a wand toward the northern sky. "We shall hunt it, we two; we shall try at the least, shall we not?" And he opened the gate, swung up to Umnik's bare back, and the bridleless horse started to move, with eyes as fixed as Ilya's, down trampled streets, past shuttered, eyeless buildings.

And the wolves fled, like the wind, which swept over the eaves and the roofs and went its way, leaving a gate banging dully.

"No," Andrei cried, but that was in his dream; and tugged at the knots, but they were sound, and the strength was gone from him, his soul fled away with the winds, where he watched all the town spread beneath him, all of Moskva embracing her knot of rivers, frozen and cracked and frozen again nigh to the bottom. He saw the gates, through a dust of blowing snow, saw old Pyotr and young Fedor's house shut up tight and the lights out. There Umnik paused, and Ilya dropped down, unbarred the gates and dragged one valve back in the obstructing snow until there was room enough for pony and rider to pass through. He climbed again to Umnik's bare back and Umnik tossed his shaggy head and jogged away in the skirl of blown snow and the glory of the northern lights. "Come back," Andrei wailed, but he spoke with the wind's voice, and the wind carried him, powerless. . . . He skimmed the surface of the snows as if his soul were a flitting bird, racing along before horse and rider, growing small again as wind swept him up. The wolves ran beside, pale movement on pale snow. . . . "They are there," he tried to shout. "Ilya, they are there."

But Ilya was no hunter to understand the bow, had not so much as strung it. Andrei swept nearer, horror in his heart, and saw Ilya's face, the image of Anna's, saw fair hair astream in the wind, snow-dusted, saw his hands . . . Ilya's delicate hands, which were his life and livelihood, bare of gloves despite the cold. And Ilya's eyes, heedless of the wolves, roved the horizon and the sky where the curtaining lights streamed and touched the snows.

Ilya rode north, and north still, with the lights ever receding to the horizon, with the wolves coursing the drifts beside, waiting their time. And the bow at last tumbled from his hand, to lie in the snow, and he never seemed to notice. The quiver slid after. "He is caught," Andrei thought, and the drawing grew dimmer and dimmer within himself, like ice melting away. Pain came back. He dreamed, helpless now, and hurting, saw Ilya slide down from Umnik's back, saw his bare hands caress the shaggy piebald coat as if in farewell, but when Ilya began to walk alone, Umnik followed after. "O go with him," Andrei wished the pony, which was part of him as Ilya had almost stopped being. "Do not let him go alone out there." And Umnik tossed his head as if, after all, he heard, and followed patiently, soundlessly in the powder snow and in the glory of the lights which played across the skies. Horror walked beside, four-footed, tongues lolling, sun-filled eyes glinting slantwise in the night, out of white, triangular faces, and teeth like shards of clear ice. Umnik threw his head and blew a frosty breath, and his eyes slowly took on that strangeness too, a sunflare gleaming, as if he were no longer one with man; and now an unsuspected enemy trod at Ilya's back.

"Ah," Andrei thought, "let me see his face," and sought in his dream to come round before him, to warn him, to tell him, to know if that same change was yet worked on him. *Ilya*, he thought with all the strength left in him. *Ilya, I am here; o look at me.*

Ilya stopped, and turned, his face only vaguely troubled, as if he had heard some strange far voice.

Ilya, o my friend.

"Andrei?" he asked, his pale lips scarcely moving, and put out his hand as if he could see him standing there. "Is it this you saw? I have never been outside the walls; I was always too sickly. But it is beautiful, Andrei."

He had no answer. The beauty which he had seen in the sky was gone; it was all dulled in his eyes, save what he saw reflected in Ilya's.

"I thought," Ilya said, "that I knew what beauty was. . . . I make beauty, Andrei, at least I thought that I made beauty; but I have never seen it until now. I should fear it, I think, but I do not. Only to kill it—Andrei, how can I? How could you?"

"Do not," he whispered. "Come back. Set me free, Ilya. Come home. Let me go."

"I have gone too far," Ilya said. "Don't look, Andrei, go back to your bed; you are dreaming. Go back."

So a dream might speak to him, his own mind's reasoning in a phantom's mouth. It made him disbelieve for a moment, and in that moment Ilya turned and walked on, toward the north. "Wait," he cried, and followed, finding it harder and harder to go, for the wind no longer carried him. "Ilya, wait."

A second time the face turned to him, still Ilya's eyes,

though unnaturally calm. And now the wolves ranged themselves upon a low ridge, slitted eyes agleam. "Come back from them," Andrei pleaded. "Do you not see them?"

Ilya looked on him with that look which he must once have turned on those who loved him, which reckoned him very distantly, and dismissed him, finding all the flaws in him.

"The wolves," he wept. "Ilya, do you not see them?"

"No," Ilya said slowly and considerately, looked about at them, and turned back. "There's nothing there. Go back. I've done this so you *could* go back, don't you understand?"

"I'll hunt them," he vowed. "I'll hunt them every one."

"No," Ilya said softly, and behind him stood the pony with eyes full of the sun; indeed the sun was rising, a thin line and bead, with glimmerings and streamings across the ice, ribbons and shafts of light which swept the snowy plain with rose and lavenders and opal odors. Ilya looked toward that sudden brilliance, turning his back. A shape was there, one with the light, robed in light, white like the snows.

"Ilya," Andrei murmured, but Ilya walked away. Andrei caught Umnik by the mane, but no more could he hold the pony . . . Umnik walked too. The wolves glided and flowed to that shape, becoming one with it, which was woman or man, and intolerably bright. "Ilya," it whispered, and opened its arms.

Andrei caught at Ilya's sleeve, and received another distant look, turned him, hugged him, to keep his face from that shape, which became woman, and chill, and ineffably beautiful. "It is your Wolf," he said, holding Ilya's face between his hands. "No more real than mine."

"As real," Ilya said. "Never less real than yours." Ilya hugged him, slightly, and without love, with only the memory of it. "You gave it what you give to beauty, Andrei; and so do I. And so do I."

He walked away, and Andrei stood, as if there were a bond holding him that had yielded all it could: he could not go further. He watched Ilya and the pony, one after the other, reach that light, saw the semblance of arms reach from it, and enfold Ilya, so that for a moment they seemed two lovers entwined; saw Umnik blurred likewise into that streaming beauty, and saw it spread with coming morning.

Of a sudden as the light came Umnik was coming back, with a rider on his back, out of the sun which streamed about him and shot rays where his hooves touched the drifts. His

rider was a like vision, in the moving of his hair and the lifting of his hand as the pony stopped . . . a fair cold face
which had been Ilya's, the hair drifting in the winds, and the
eyes, the eyes ablaze with opal gold, like lamps making his
glowing face dark.

"Come," Ilya whispered. "O my friend."

Andrei turned and fled, raced with the retreating night, fled
with other shadows, mounted the winds, naked and alone. He
crossed the rivers, and saw the bridge, saw Moskva embracing the frozen ice with its wooden walls, and staining the pu-
rity of the world with its dark buildings. He found the open
gate and whisked in, skimmed the well-trodden street, found
the least chink in the wall of the house and gained entry, into
warmth and stillness, into the loft, where he rested, trapped
as before.

He woke, turned his head, found the place by him empty.

"Ilya!" he cried, and woke the house.

They found him by the gate, by the corner of the front-
yard fence, partly covered by the blowing snow, frozen and
with tiny ice crystals clinging to clothes and face . . . not terrible, as some of the dead were which the cold killed, but
rather as one gazing into some fair dream, and smiling. Andrei touched his face as Anna held him, shedding tears which
melted ice upon his cheek; and suddenly in his agony he
sprang up and ran to the stable, with the others calling out
after him.

Umnik lay there, quite stiff and dead. The other pony
looked at him reproachfully, and the goats bleated, and he
turned away, walked back to the others, gathered Anna into
his arms.

The spring was then not long in coming; the winds shifted
and the snows shrank and the rivers began to groan with
breaking ice.

Andrei rode the other pony in the trodden street, the bay,
the younger, a beast which would never be what Umnik had
been. The drifts within the city yielded up the white wind-
blasted pillars which had been statues, turned up small and
pitiful discoveries, small animals which had been frozen the
winter long; and an old woman had been found near the
Moskva river. But such tragedies came with every winter; and
spring came and the white retreated.

He passed the gates and the bridge, and neglected his eye-shields as he rode along. He had a new bow and quiver . . . the old ones, from Ilya's dead hand, had seemed unlucky to him . . . and he rode out along the edge of the retreating woods, where trees shed their burdens of snow, where the tracks of deer were visible.

He and Anna had begun their living together before the spring; he wore work of her stitchery, and she swelled with child, and the dull scar of winter past seemed bearable. He had taken a free gift to the old wizard, Mischa, who had now lived yet another winter—a pair of fat hares, paying for truth he had gotten, and bearing no resentments.

The bay pony's hooves broke melting snow, cracked ice, and there was a glistening on it from the sun, but the day was still overcast. He shielded his eyes with a gloved hand and looked at the drifts of gray-centered cloud, shivered somewhat later as the cloud blew athwart the sun, and a chill came into the air.

There were only ordinary days, forever. He saw the places in Moskva where the paint peeled, saw cracks in the images of Moskva; the patterns which Anna made to clothe him seemed garish and far less lovely than once they had; he had seen beauty once, and aimed at it and wounded it.

Now he saw truth.

"Was it your sight you gave the Wolf?" he had asked Mischa finally. "Or was it the hand?"

"I destroyed my sight," Mischa had said, "—after."

Mischa had had no one. He had three families; had Anna; had a growing child.

Had had a friend.

Ilya's carvings faded; would crack; would decay with the age of Moskva. Ilya had made nothing lasting. Nor did any man.

The colors would fade and the ice would come; he knew that, but looked at the colors and the patterns men made, because he had seared the other from his heart and from his eyes; and he went on looking at it because others needed him.

Cold touched the side of his face and pushed at his body, a touch of deep chill, a breathing of sleet and snowflakes. The bay pony threw her head and snorted in unease.

What had Ilya seen? he wondered again and again. What, if not the Wolf?

What had it been, that drew him away?

Snowflakes dusted the pony's black mane, smallish stars, each different, each delicate and white and in the world's long age, surely duplicated again and again. As human grief was.

He looked toward the north, toward the gleam of ice and sunlight, opal and orange and rose and gold, melting-bright.

There was nothing there.

Forever.

NIGHTGAME

(Rome)

They offered him food and drink. He accepted, although by all his codes he should not. He was no one. They had taken his name with his totem and his weapons, and they had killed Ta'in, who was his heart. A warrior of the *netang*, he would have refused food and drink offered from an enemy's hand, and died of it, but they had forced it into him during the long traveling that had brought him to this place, and taken from him all that he was, and he was tired. His weapons, had he had them, could never have fought the like of them, with their machines and their mocking smiles. He would have killed them all if he could, but that was while he had been a warrior, and while he had had a name. Now he sat listlessly and waited what more would happen, and what he would be, which was something of their purposing.

Belat switched the vid off and smiled at the portly executive who rested in the bowl-chair in the offices of the Earth Trade Center, next the crumbling port. "*Netang* tribesman, off Phoenix IV. That's what I've gotten us."

Ginar folded his hands across his paunch and nodded slowly to Belat the trader. Grinned, in rising amusement. "The Tyrant will be vastly surprised. You go as planned . . . tonight?"

"I've advised the usual contacts," Belat said, "that I have a special surprise for the evening. I've permission to cross the bridge. I even detected a spark of enthusiasm."

"A special surprise." Ginar chuckled again. It would be that. "You'll not," he said, "mention *my* name in the City, as sponsor of this . . . should something go wrong. *Your* risk.

After all—it's your risk. I only provide you . . . opportunity."

The city was old as Earth was old, in the waning chill of its plague-spotted sun.

The Eternal City . . . under the latest of its many names, in the reign of the latest of its tyrants. It sat on its seven hills by its sluggish, miasmic river, and dreamed dreams.

That was the passion of its Tyrant, and of all the nobles of the city—dreams. The apparatus (which might have originated here, or perhaps on one of the colonial worlds: no one remembered) existed in the Palace which dominated the city; it gave substance to dreams, and by that substance consoled the violet nights and the oppressive days of the sickly star. There was nothing left to *do* on Earth, nothing at all, for the vanities were all exposed, the ambitions, the conceits of empire, the meaningless nature of power on one world, when greater powers now spanned the void and embraced worlds in the plural, when those powers themselves had had time to grow old and to decay many times. Earth had seen it all. The Eternal City had seen such eras pass . . . too often to be amused by the exercise of power or the pursuit of empire. It had no hopes left, being merely old, as the sun was old, and the moon looming large and sickly in the sky, lurid with the reflected glow of the ailing sun. Earth and the City could have no ambitions. Ambitions were for younger worlds. For the City there was only pleasure.

And the dreaming.

Exquisite decadence, the dreams . . . in which some lost themselves and failed to return—dreams which, in the strange power of the machine, could become too real, which for those that fell too far within their power wrought real consequences on fleshly bodies.

The days the Eternal City gave to mundane pursuits, for those who waked . . . the supervision of the dullard laborers who toiled in the catacomb depths of the City. The sun was a fearsome thing, and during most of the day the City stirred only beneath the ground, in the far-reaching windings of the tunnels, where mushrooms grew, and blind fishes, and yeasts and other such things; and by mornings and evenings, when the sun was kinder, the laborers tended the crops which still flourished on the edges of the sluggish River. Such men chose to work, and not to dream, amid the fearsome cruelties of

their lords. The day belonged to them, and to the lesser
nobles whose tedious duty it was to oversee, and to tally, and
to arrange trade with the few ships which might chance to
touch at the port across the River. The City had some mundane concerns, and labor existed, not because it had to, but
because some men knew themselves doomed to be victims,
and knew themselves less imaginative, and less fierce, and
made themselves beasts of burden, because beasts toiled their
little share and so fed themselves and so lived. Such were the
days of the City.

But the nights, the violet nights . . . then, up on the
Palace hill, the delicate dreamers sank into the many-colored
deviances, the eldritch pleasures, the past of the City which
had been, empires long lost—the past which might have been;
the true future and the future which could never be.

The City exported dreams. This alone was enough to sus-
tain its nobles, the glittering crowd which attended on the
Tyrant. They dreamed; and when it pleased them, they sold
those dreams, recorded tapes of a flavor and nature which
alone could satisfy the jaded dreamtrippers of the Limb's dec-
adent First Colonies (where law had long ago faded) or the
illicit trade on younger worlds elsewhere. They were a commodity unique among expensive vices . . . expensive because
they came from Earth, which was remote from important
worlds; because they were rare (seldom would the Tyrant
consent); and because they were purchased with lives.

The Port of the City remained open for this trade alone,
bringing in the mere food and drink and precious objects
which kept the nobles of the City well-disposed and luxuri-
ous—bringing in, more rarely, that prize victim which could
open the iron gates of the seventh hill, and secure a tape of
such sport as would echo wealth across the stars, enriching
the hands through which it passed.

Hence Ginar, who lived in affluence in his mansion by the
port, served by countless servants who found tending Ginar
more comfortable than toiling for the lords of the City . . .
lapped in the luxury of goods he siphoned off from those
lords, who hardly missed them. Presidency of such a post had
to offer some recompense in luxury, physically, for it meant
exile from the civilized worlds, the young worlds, where life
was, and some could not have endured that. But there was
one luxury Ginar had here, besides his fine foods and his servants: he was himself of one of the First Colonies, and for

many years he had been an addict, a dreamtripper, who lived
for that pleasure which was nearer here than anywhere—and
across the River, out of reach save when some tape could be
brought from out of the City, bought at price.

Hence Belat, who made the long ship runs, who had been
very long in the trade, and whose well-being presently
trembled on the brink.

Belat started now across the bridge, when the sun was still
at dawning, and safe—across the bridge which was the oldest
and the last of the bridges of the City. On it, monoliths which
had been statues stared down, marble pillars deprived by time
of all feature, only hints of faces, like wide-mouthed screams
and sunken eyes, and handless, outstretched arms.

And beyond that . . . a slow walk through the City itself,
through the catacombs, which were ruin piled on ruin, untend-
ed, for no one cared to repair what time had always, eter-
nally, destroyed. Workers stared from eyes like those of the
statues, pits of shadow, fear-haunted. Sometimes one would
dart away, but most would stand wherever they were caught,
trying, perhaps, to seem dull—for nightly what time there
was no special game, the lords walked out among them and
chose one of them for that fate, whatever one the lords
judged guilty of imagination, whatever one promised sport.

He never saw one defiant. Those who offered such looks
would have been first chosen, most savored.

He walked on, paying no great attention to them, not liking their eyes; he never had, in the many times he had
walked this path.

Seven hills, and the centermost was a cloven hill, where
lightnings played most frequently in storms, a hill poised
above ruins and split by the seam of an ancient fault. Gods
had dwelt here once, and now the Tyrant did, at the end of a
road which walked the ancient line of destruction, sleeping
now, as the City slept, huddled on its hills. In this place had
been an ancient ruin, and bits of white marble worked up
like broken bone from the seam of this old wound, the only
bare ground in all the City, surrounded by catacombs, the
heaped up ruins of the millennia of the City's old age.

An iron gate began that valley, where a Keeper stood, a
lesser lord, on daywatch, with a shelter from the sun when it
should rise, a gatehouse of jumbled bits of marble, aged and
smooth, and twined about with vines. The Keeper's interest

pricked at this visitation—which came but so very seldom, and Belat stood before the gates without touching them, hands folded, matching the hauteur of the guard himself.

"I've a gift," Belat said. The Keeper regarded him a moment more from kohl-rimmed eyes, gave a languid, deadly smile.

And with a touch the young lord loosed the gate. "Go on," he whispered, in that hoarse, hushed tone of the aristocracy of the City. None of the nobles spoke loudly; it was the mark of their peculiar art.

He passed through, walked that way among the ruins. He felt the smile behind his back, a feral smile which followed him with lazy, kohl-rimmed eyes, and lusted for him, in one way or the other.

The road wound on, over that field of broken bits of antiquity, with the catacombs looming down on the left, with a slow tide of them seeming to lap at this valley on his right. The road wound, for no apparent reason, but there might have been, once, in the long ago past, buildings which lay buried now. The Games were very old here. It was told that this place had known man's oldest and most dire vices, the ultimate sport of a species once hunters . . . to hunt itself.

"I've a gift," he informed the Keeper of the second gate, who stood behind the iron grill, before a gatehouse likewise sheltered from the sun. Behind this rose the Way of a Thousand Steps, and the inmost gates. "Then," that one whispered, opening wide the gates, "there will be a good hunt tonight, won't there?"

He climbed on, panting now, and with a weakness in his knees that was not all his lack of exercise, his habitude of ships. Above him the Lotus Dome of the palace loomed against the morning, far, far up the steps worn into hollows by the passage of feet, of the Keepers up and down, and of the victims . . . up.

"I've a gift," he informed the Keeper of the third gate, the very doors.

That one merely grinned, showing sharp blue teeth, and let him pass.

Belat walked on, into the long inner halls of lotus-stem columns, which twisted their way up and writhed across vaulted ceilings; and far, into yet another hall, where the stems rose to stone lily pads and marble lotuses on the ceiling, stems behind which coy golden-scaled fishes lurked . . .

beneath which a throne like one alabaster lotus flower, and languid golden limbs disposed upon it, and dark, kohl-smeared eyes regarding him. The Tyrant frowned at him, a cloud upon the youthful brow, a sudden quick movement of a jewel-nailed hand, a gesture to begone—mercy now twice given. Twelve years old was Elio DCCLII, petulant, spoiled . . . dangerous. "Go away," the boy whispered, "—*foreigner*. We sent you away last time. Do you think we forget? Do you think we forgive?"

"I've brought you a gift," Belat said, and watched the old interest grow unwillingly in the Tyrant's eyes . . . interests like pleasures which quickly came and quickly fled, which made this handsome, golden child the ruler he was—most skilled of dreamers, worker of finesses and deadly dangers the most jaded could not match, a coolness which insulated him from shocks and let him shape the dreams his way. Assassinations had been tried before—in vain.

"Your last gift," the boy said, "failed."

"This one," Belat said, venturing a step closer, "this one will not."

"What have you brought us?" the boy-Tyrant whispered, leaning forward on the Lotus Throne. "Something—new?"

"A dreamer," Belat whispered back, and before the pouting, painted lips could frame a word . . . "A *different* dreamer. A wild dreamer. Something you've not hunted, majesty, something Earth has never seen."

The familiar petulance trembled on the childish lips, the frown gathered, deadly shadow in the kohl-smeared eyes . . . fresh from the night's hunt was Elio, and perhaps sated, or perhaps—disappointed. "You mean to stay," the Tyrant lisped, "and record this . . . with your machines. We should submit to this—distasteful intrusion in our sport. And you *sell* these things, do you not?"

"I have to travel far," he said, cautious on this point. "Consider only, majesty, that I search the worlds for you . . . to bring you such a gift. And the record makes it possible again."

"You intrude."

"Don't I bring you the rarest treasures, majesty? Can the dull creatures out there match mine? Don't I bring you always the most unusual, the greatest sport?"

"You *bored* us, dream-stealer. You raised our hopes, and you failed them, and are there not others—seller of our pleasures—who would fill your place more cleverly? Ships would still come and go at the port. The factor would still be there. And perhaps the next trader would be more careful . . . might he not? You *bored* us. So long we waited for what you promised, and it *failed*. We let you go once. Not again."

Belat sweated, resisted temptation to mop at his face and admit it. Ruin was on the one side. On the other—"You'll take my gift," he whispered. "It's my expense, majesty. And if it pleases, the tape . . . to take with me."

"I'll take it," the boy said ever so softly. "And let you make your tape; but, Belat, this time there will be no forgiving. We'll hunt *you* if it fails to please."

He shivered, stared into the boyish eyes, and hated, smothering that hate, striving to smile. "I am confident," he said. "Would I risk coming here again—without cause to be?"

The eyes took on suspicion, the least suspicion, quickly fled, and a childish hand waved him gone. Belat took his cue, gathered his life and his sanity into his two hands and walked velvet footed from the lotus-stem hall—walked the long way down, past curiosity borning in the Keepers' eyes, curiosity which itself was, in the Eternal City, a commodity precious more than gold.

The sun climbed higher, and outside, the City sank into its daytime burrowings; and the Lotus Palace sank into its daily hush. Elio bathed, a lingering immersion in a golden bowl only slightly more gleaming than the limbs which curled in it, serpent-lithe and slender. He walked the cool, lily-stemmed halls, and stared restlessly out upon the only unshielded view in the Palace, upon the ruin-flecked valley below the hill, upon the catacombs sheened by the daystar's terrible radiations, and behind him his attendant lesser lords observed this madness with languid-lidded eyes, hoping for something bizarre. But he was not struck by the sun, nor did he leap to his death, as four Tyrants before him had done, when amusements failed; and he turned on them a look which in itself gave them a prized thrill of terror . . . remembering that to assuage the pangs of the last failed hunt—a minor lord had fallen to him in the Games, rare, rare sport.

But he passed them by with that deadly look and walked on, absorbed in his anticipations, often raised, ever disappointed.

The kill was always too swift. And he knew the whispers,

that such power as his always burned itself out, that it grew more and more inward, lacking challenge, until at last nothing should suffice to stir him.

He imagined. Such talent was rare. The sickness was on him, that came on the talented, the brilliant dreamers, who found no further challenges. At twelve, he foresaw a day not far removed when his own death would seem the only excitement yet untried. He knew the halls, each lotus stem and startled, golden fish. He knew the lords and ladies, knew them, not alone the faces, but the very souls, and drank in all their pleasures, fed by them, nourished on their darkest fantasies, and was bored.

He probed the deaths of victims, and found even that tedious.

He grew thin, pacing the halls by day, and exhausting his body in dreams at night.

He terrorized captured laborers, but that waking sport palled, for the dreams were more, and deeper, and more colorful, unlimited in fantasy, save by the limits of the mind.

And these he had paced and plumbed as well.

At twelve he knew the limits of all about him, and had experienced all the pleasures, heritor of a thousand thousands of his sort, all of whom died young, in a City which found its Eternity a slow, slow death.

Perhaps tonight, he thought, savoring the thought, I die.

He sat much, in the cell. This day—if it was day—he knew that they were watching him, and they had not, before. This they were free to do, and he could not protest. He sat, and stared at his hands, and waited. There would come a time that they would insist he must eat and drink; or they would make him sleep and force this upon him. He sat still now, not betraying that he knew that they were there. He had had dignity once. They had none, who peeped and pried and did not come before his face, but that was his shame, who had fallen to the like of these. One day they must tire of this, he thought, when he let himself think at all, and then they must decide what they would do. Perhaps today, he thought, but did not let himself hold that thought, for that was ultimately to put himself in their power, and he would neither react nor think of them. He was alone. They had made him so. More than this they had to come and do to him. He would not help them.

And then the weariness came on his limbs, and he sat, still possessed of his little dignity, while his limbs loosed, and he began to yield. They did this to him when they wished to handle him. They wished so now.

But this time the limbs alone failed, and consciousness did not.

The dying sun was sinking, and the engorged moon rose over the marshes by the river, touched the catacombs of the common hills and the Lotus Dome of the seventh.

It was the hour.

The procession left the port, a slow line of the servants of Ginar, bearing the recording devices, bearing a black plastic coffin. They crossed the bridge of featureless statues; by the time the last rim of the diseased sun was sinking, they were treading the ways of the catacombs, where laborers watched like statues, fearing, perhaps, for the direst dreams sometimes spilled beyond, and worked terror even here, a miasma from the Palace that infected even the City.

They reached the first of the gates, and crossed the field of ruin; reached the second, and passed to the Way of the Thousand Steps, and up that height to the third. There the servants stayed, and set down the apparatus, and the coffin. Belat took up the apparatus, struggling with the weight; the Keepers and lords took up the coffin and bore it further, within the forbidden perimeters of the Lotus Palace, where only the privileged might go.

And victims.

Some, brought here, struggled at the last; some cried or cursed. This one did not, drugged, but not too far: Belat was sure of that. The coffin went ahead through the lotus-stem hall, and Belat walked last, incongruously like a mourner, head bowed with his load, panting after the measured steps of the Keepers who bore the case—into the inmost hall, of the lily-pad ceiling and the Lotus Throne.

The dreams were prepared. The apparatus which *was* the Lotus Dome was soon to be engaged. And the Tyrant would have his precious surprise, a manic *netang* . . . a trap neatly laid, even legally: a primitive mind this, without the softness of the dreamtrippers who were his usual gifts, the addicts of the First Colonies who fell into his hands and disappeared, seeking the ultimate thrill—and finding it here, themselves become material for the City and its dreams, recorded, sold in turn, to lure others.

Not this time . . . this time a surprise for his majesty Elio DCCLII, one which might serve a double turn. Belat's breath came short with more than the burden he carried, and his skin had a deathly clamminess; he grinned, a grimace round his panting—for it was the Tyrant who was the focus of the dreams, the Tyrant who led . . . who died, if things went wrong.

Revenge, on the one hand, for the terrors he had suffered; and most of all—a new Tyrant to trade with, one more manageable, whereby he could keep his post. No more threats. No more humiliations. There were no more talents such as Elio's here—or the earlier assassinations would have succeeded. A manageable tyrant . . . well worth the price and risk.

Or on the other hand . . . *gratitude,* if that word had currency here. Pleasure, a hunt the Tyrant would much savor. And ask another, and another, until he died.

In either case a dream of special flavor, a unique prize which was his alone. Delicious murder, the wild *netang* with his savagery among these hunters, primitive innocence loosed among the jaded minds of the oldest city of man . . .

Or the death of a Tyrant of this city, with all its sensitive agonies, for when Elio should falter, they would all turn on him, all.

And the machines would capture it for him.

There was no fighting, as there had been none before. They bore him where they chose, to do what they chose. He wept in his narrow prison . . . not violent weeping, only the helpless flow of a tear down his cheek, but his body was paralyzed and he could not wipe it away. It shamed him, but he had encountered many shames since he lost his name and himself.

He felt movement, knew himself carried, had perceived them near water, in a closed echoing place, climbing . . . perhaps to hurl him to his death; but that seemed a small act after all the others. Now he heard echoes as of some great cavern . . . smelled thick scents of rot and of flowers, where before the climbing the air had been cold and clean.

Perhaps he had already died. He was no longer sure.

Belat bowed, smiled at the great Tyrant, who lounged on
the Lotus Throne, in the inmost chamber of stone flowers.
The whole court was about him, fantastical in their array,
their painted skins and kohl-rimmed eyes, their nodding
plumes and gossamer robes . . . like living flowers about the
stone lotus-stems and golden fishes.

The boy Tyrant moved his fingers, which flashed amethyst
from jeweled nails. The Keepers set down the coffin before
him on the floor, opened it, exposing the brown, still body
within. A whisper of displeasure went up, disappointment,
but the tribesman's eyes opened, and glared, and a titter of
anticipation ran round the room. Elio leaned forward on his
throne, elbow against a lily-petal arm, chin propped on fist.
His amethyst-dusted lids blinked; rouged lips smiled; and
Belat who had gone rigid with fear—relaxed and smiled as
well. The Tyrant flicked that look in his drection and the
smile froze.

"The agreement, majesty."

"Haste," the boy said.

Belat made haste, found himself a corner the disdainful
lords and ladies allowed, set up his recorder, hands trembling
in anxiety. He did not share the dreams—observed only.

When he had made the few adjustments, he made feverish
speed to shield himself, to inject into his veins a stimulant
that would keep him as much as possible—awake. He observed. When he entered into the dreams at all, it was always
as a mere spectator, distant: he was not, himself, an addict.
He preserved that remoteness as he valued his life, for the
dreamtrippers were not without humor.

Elio smiled, amethyst-lidded eyes intent upon his prize.
Others of his lords and ladies gathered close about him, a
pastel ring of painted faces intent to stare at the tribesman
within his coffin, savoring what they saw.

The boy Tyrant moved his hand once. The lights in all the
dome dimmed. A second gesture. The apparatus engaged.

He stood. He could move again, and that sudden freedom
shocked him. He was knee-deep, naked, in rotting marsh. The
whole world was flat and the sun was barely able to provide
a murky twilight.

"It's the end of the world," a voice whispered within him.
"Where all the land has worn away. It's *old*."

A bird hovered against the sickly disc of the sun, watching.

He tried to walk, but there was nowhere to walk to, for the marsh stretched as far as the eye could see in all directions, and he had no memory of how he had got there. The flatness was sinister. He walked toward the sun, that being the only object there was in all the world, walked until he tired, and stopped, still knee-deep in water.

A movement brushed against his ankle. He started and looked down. A serpent with amethyst scales, bright in all that brown, wound round his calf and lifted its head against his thigh—stared at him with wise and knowing eyes.

"I am young," it said.

No, he thought, refusing such madness, and it was a brown bit of weed.

He stood in a cave, where water dripped in blackness. He moved, and his steps echoed in far darkness. The cold bit into him. There was water before his feet, and fish hung glowing in it, and upon the wall, a worm spun a glowing web.

"It's the heart of the world," the voice whispered. "And it's hollow."

Water fell, plopped in tinkling echoes. Something moved, and breathed, and came toward him, dragging vast bulk among the rocks, which rattled and shifted in the dark.

"I have no heart," it said.

No, he thought again, but he would not run, and light broke about him, white and blinding.

He stood atop a mountain higher than all mountains, in snow, with mountain peaks about it, thrusting out of cloud; and the sun turned red and stained the white with blood. The bird was back, an inky blot, hovering on rowing wings against the gales which shook his naked limbs and streamed his hair into his eyes. The winds turned warm. He looked about him, and a languor stole over him.

"It's the height of the world," the voice whispered. "The sky is very near this place."

The warmth increased, melting down the drifts, and a woman lay naked in the snow, violet-lidded and seeming asleep. Her eyes began to open.

No, he thought at once, for he trusted nothing in this place. The lips parted and laughed; and the sleeper became a grinning skull, became a beast, became woman and man and goddess and god, became a machine which walked in the likeness of a man, and a demon which at last became the serpent again, and danced for him, hood spread, tongue flickering, violet-scaled against the ruddy snow.

"I am desire," it said, hissing. In the clouds about the peak, towers rose, and became what he knew for a city, and time flowed backward into an ancient past, of wars and armies and conquests, of horrors and of greatness of its kings. All of this he was offered, and all the while the black bird hovered in the winds. White beasts had gathered, and there came a faint, threatening laughter.

"Run," they taunted him. He tried to stand, but he was a beast hooved and made to be their prey. He whirled on slender legs, stretched out and ran, and they howled after him, across the snow, among the rocks. He skidded on ice, recovered and ran, bursting his heart in his running, leaping and bounding where he might till the air tore his lungs and his belly ached, till limbs quivered with the shocks of his leaps and he ran slower and slower, among crags echoing with laughter. The rocks closed before him, a cul de sac. He turned, his four legs trembling, and lowered his horned head, gasping.

But they were men, like those of the ancient city, and bore bows. They pierced him with arrows and his blood stained the snow and the rocks and ran in great smears down the sky.

No! he thought, refusing to die. He looked up at the bird which was always there, and saw among the rocks the violet-eyed serpent, which coiled with head uplifted, watching him.

It shaped itself. He made up his mind and did the same. He was a man again, on two feet. The bird screamed in the sky, and he gave it a cold look, and healed himself of his wounds. He glanced again at the serpent, but a whole host of polychrome serpents had taken its place, and the rocks had acquired a pair of eyes, amethyst-rimmed.

They were lively with interest. "What is your name?" the voice asked.

He shaped his totem again. It hung about his neck. He drew a great breath, suffused with power, and named them his name. He extended the ground at his feet, and made it golden grass, stretched it wide and pushed back the mountain peaks, until his own mountains stood there again. He made the sky blue overhead, and the sun, young and yellow. He stretched wide his arms, embracing the world, and looked again toward the rocks. A naked boy stood there, among the serpents, which hissed and threatened. The boy looked frightened, a frowning, sullen fear, with will to fight. He approved that, respected it.

"Elio," he said, for he knew that name among the others. He ignored the frown and made game in the land, and more and better birds to fly in the heavens, made the great river, and fish to swim in it, made it all as it had been, and himself as he had been, and lifted his hand and looked about him, showing it all to the boy who was a king.

"*No!*" the bird cried; and the serpents, far away now, wove into a man of metal which started at the horizon and clicked toward them.

"They will kill you," the boy said. "They will kill me too if I stand here. Let me out of your dream. Let me go. I should not have stepped so far apart from them."

"Do you want to leave?" he asked the boy, who, naked, looked about at the blue sky and the bright young sun and all the grasslands, and shook his head, his eyes shining violet to the depths.

"It is young," he said. "What else is it?"

He shut his eyes a moment, and dreamed Ta'in, whose vast slit eyes and scaly nose took shape for him, head and great amber-scaled body . . . huge, fierce Ta'in, who had carried *him* from boyhood. The dragon rubbed against him and nosed the boy, lifted a wide slit-eyed gaze at the edge of the land, which with every step of the metal creature, turned to metal and cities, and over that creeping change, a ship hovered, bristling with offworlders' weapons.

"We must run," the boy said.

He paid no heed, swung up to Ta'in's back, faced the metal edge which was growing wider and nearer, and reckoned well that this was the last time, that if he lost Ta'in again, Ta'in was truly lost, and so was he. He had his weapons again, drew bow and fired at the advancing edge, fired shaft after shaft, and saw the machines and the guns bearing down on him as they had before.

He was not alone. Another dragon whipped up beside him, with a young rider in the saddle. The boy drew bow and fired, shouted for joy to see the metal edge retreat ever so slightly.

And then there was another dragon, and another rider, on the boy's left.

"Mahin!" the boy cried, naming him. Three bows launched

arrows now, and yet for all they took back, the metal edge still struggled forward.

And stopped its advance, for another and another dragon appeared, a hissing thunder. He saw them, shrieked a war cry, ordered attack, and the riders were still joining them, while dragon bodies surged forward, and Ta'in's power rippled between his knees. The arrows became a storm. The metal edge retreated, and the ship, last of all, began to shiver in a sky gone blue, plummeted down, grew feathers, shed them and died.

He looked about him, at the bright familiar land, at the keen-eyed warriors who had joined him, men and women, at the brave boy who was his once-lost son. Pride welled up in him.

"Your dream," his son said, love burning in his eyes, "is best of all."

"Let me in," Ginar said. He had walked far to the iron gates, and his bulk made walking difficult. Two days and Belat had not returned. It was a desperate act, to cross the bridge unbidden, to venture the catacombs . . . all but deserted now, but he had seen the movement from the hill by the port, the drift of peasants going where they would not have dared to go, the gradual desertion of the fringes of the city, the long silence . . . and Ginar, who was an addict of the dream, could no longer bear the question. "Let me in," he begged of the Keeper, who did not *look* like the legendary Keepers, but more like one of the peasants. He hoped for the tape at least, to have that, to savor the dream for which he had been longing with feverish desire.

The Keeper let him in. He walked, panting, the long road through the field of ruin, where peasants sat with placid eyes. Walked, with long, painful pauses, to the inner gates, and found them open; climbed, which took him very long, the Way of the Thousand Steps, sweating and panting; but he was driven by his addiction, and not by any rational impulse. Belat had promised him—promised him the most unique of all dreams. He had imagined this, savored this, desired it with a desire that consumed all sense . . . to have this one greatest dream . . . to experience such a death, and live—

At long last he reached the doors, which stood ajar, where peasants sat along the corridors . . . he stumbled among their bodies, pushed and forced his way in gathering shadow, for the lamps were dimmed. He entered the lotus hall at last, where peasants sat among the lords of dream, where a boy sat on a flower throne.

And a weariness came on his limbs so that they could no longer move, for it was night and the dream was strong. He sank down, no longer conscious of his bulk, forgetful of such desires, and the pleasures he had come to find.

He sat down in the council ring among the tents, and smiled, while the dragons stamped and shuffled outside the camp, and the wind whispered in the grass beyond, and the three moons were young.

HIGHLINER

(New York City)

The city soared, a single spire aimed at the clouds, concave-curved from sprawling base to needle heights. It had gone through many phases in its long history. Wars had come and gone. Hammered into ruin, it rebuilt on that ruin, stubbornly rising as if up were the only direction it knew. How it had begun to build after that fashion no one remembered, only that it grew, and in the sun's old age, when the days of Earth turned strange, it grew into its last madness, becoming a windowed mountain, a tower, a latter-day Babel aimed at the sullen heavens. Its expanse at the base was enormous, and it crumbled continually under its own weight, but its growth outpaced that ruin, growing broader and broader below and more and more solid at its base and core, with walls crazily angled to absorb the stresses.

Climate had changed many times over the course of its life. Ice came now and froze on its crest, and even in summers, evening mists iced on the windward side, crumbling it more; but still it grew, constantly webbed with scaffolding at one point or the other, even at the extreme heights; and the smaller towers of its suburbs followed its example, so that on its peripheries, bases touching and joining its base, strange concave cones lifted against the sky, a circle of spires around the greater and impossible spire of the City itself, on all sides but the sea.

At night the City and its smaller companions gleamed with lighted windows, a spectacle the occupants of the outlying city-mountains could see from their uppermost windows, looking out with awe on the greatest and tallest structure man had ever built on Earth . . . or ever would. And from the much higher windows of the City itself, the occupants might look out on a perspective to take the senses away, towering over all the world. Even with windows tinted and shielded against the dying sun's radiations, the reflections off the surface of the land and the windows of other buildings flared and glared with disturbing brightness; and by night the cities rose like jeweled spires of the crown of the world, towering mounds which one day might be absorbed as their bases had already been.

It was alone, the City and its surrounding companions, on a land grown wild between; on an Earth severed from the younger inhabited worlds, with its aged and untrustworthy star.

The tower was for the elite, the artists, the analysts, the corporate directors and governors; the makers and builders and laborers lived at the sprawling, labyrinthine base, and worked there, in the filling of the core, or outward, in the quarrying of still more and more stone which came up the passages, from sources ever farther away; and some worked the outer shell, adding to it. It was mountain and city at once; and powerful yet. It had pride, in the hands of its workers and the soaring height of it.

And the highliners walked with a special share of that pride, proud in their trade and in the badges of it, among which were a smallish size and a unique courage.

Johnny and Sarah Tallfeather were such, brother and sister; and Polly Din and Sam Kenny were two others. They were of the East Face, of the 48th sector (only they worked everywhere) and when they were at the Bottom, in the domain of the Builders, they walked with that special arrogance of their breed, which could hang suspended on a thread in the great cold winds of Outside, and look down on the city-mountains, and wield a torch or manage the erection of the cranes, which had to be hoisted up from the smallest web of beginning lines and winches, which, assembled, hoisted up more scaffolding and stone and mortar. They could handle vast weights in the winds by patience and skill, but most of all, they could dare the heights and the ledges.

Others might follow them, on the platforms they made, creep about on those platforms anchored by their lines, Builders brave enough compared to others, who found it all their hearts could bear just to go up above the two hundreds and look down from the outershell windows; but those who worked the high open face on lines alone were a special breed, the few who could bear that fearful fascination, who could work between the dying sun and the lesser cities, who could step out on nothing and swing spiderwise in the howling winds and freezing mists; and rarer still, those with the nerve and with the skill of engineers as well. They were the first teams on any site, the elite of a special breed.

That was the 48th.

The order was out: the city would grow eastward, toward the Queens Tower; the work was well under way, the Bottom skylights covered on that side, because the high work required it. There was a burst of prosperity in the eastside Bottom, establishments which fed and housed the Builders who were being shifted there.

"It's going to *change,*" some higher up muttered, less happy, for it meant that favorite and favored real estate would lose its view, and accesses, pass into the core, ultimately to be filled, and their windows would be taken out and carefully, lovingly transferred to the Outside as the building progressed: the computers ruled, dictated the cost-effective procedures; and the highliners moved in.

They began by walking the lower levels, work which made them impatient, mostly leaving that to Builders, who were skilled enough; then their real work began, mounting the East Face itself, floor by floor, swinging out in the winds and seeking with their eyes for any weaknesses in structure or stone which deviated from what the computers predicted. Small cracks were abundant and ordinary; they noted them on charts and the regular liner crews would fill them.

The liners worked higher and higher; came to the Bottom each night in increasing numbers, for the scaffolding had begun now, far across the Bottom, and new joy dens and sleeps had opened up to accommodate them in the sprawl of the base.

There were of course deeper levels than the liners ever saw: and they too were worked by a special breed that was doing its own job, men who probed the foundations which were going to bear that new weight, who crawled the narrow tunnels still left deep in the stonework heart of the base. Rivers, it was rumored, still flowed down there, but long ago the City had enclosed them, channeled them, dug down to rock beneath and settled her broad bottomside against the deep rocks, perched there for the ages to come. That great weight cracked supports from time to time, and precious conduits of power and water had to be adjusted against the sideways slippage which did happen, fractional inches year by year, or sometimes more, when the earth protested the enormous weight it had to bear. The sea was down there on one side, but those edges were filled and braced; the dead were down there, the ashes of all the ordinary dead, and many a Builder too, who had not gotten out of the way of a collapsing passage . . . but the dead served like other dust, to fill the cracks, so it was true that the living built upon the dead.

So the city grew.

"Go up to the nineties tomorrow," the liner boss said, and the four other members of 48 East, tired from the day and bone-chilled from the mist and anxious to head for the Bottom and its dens, took Jino Brown's instructions and handed in their charts. "So where were you, bossman?" Sam Kenny asked. Sometimes Jino went out with them and sometimes not; and it was a cold, bone-freezing day out there.

"Yeah," said Johnny. "The wind starts up, Jino, and where were you?"

"Meeting," Jino said; fill-in for their retired boss, he took such jokes with a sour frown, not the good humor they tried with him. "Yor worry too much," Johnny said, and unbelted the harness about his hips, last in, still shivering and bouncing to warm his muscles. He started peeling out of the black rubber suit, hung up his gear beside the others in the narrow Access Room, with the big hatch to Outside firmly and safely sealed at the end; they had a shower there: Sarah and Poll had first use of it. They came out looking happier and Johnny peeled out of the last of his rig, grabbed a towel and headed in with Sam, howled for the temperature the women had left it, which on their chilled bodies felt scalding. Sam dialed it down, and they lathered and soused themselves and came out again, rubbing down.

The women were dressed already, waiting. "Where's Jino gone now?" Sam asked. The women shrugged.

"Got to be careful of him," Sarah said. "Think we hurt his feelings."

"Ah," Johnny said, which was what that deserved. He grabbed his clothes and pulled them on; and Sam did, while the women waited. Then, "Going Down," Sarah sang, linking her arm in his, linking left arm to Sam's and laughing; he snagged Polly and they snaked their way out and down the hall, laughing for the deviltry of it, here in this carpeted, fine

place of the tower, quiet, expensive apartments of the
Residents. They used the service lift, their privilege . . . better, because *it* stopped very seldom, and not at all this time,
shot them down and down while they leaned against the walls
and grinned at each other in anticipation.

"Worm," Sarah proposed, a favorite haunt.

"Pillar," Poll said.

"Go your way; we'll go ours."

"Right," Sam said; and that was well enough: Sam and
Sarah had business; and he and Poll did, and he was already
thinking on it with a warm glow . . . on that and dinner,
both of which seemed at the moment equally desirable. The
lift slammed to its hard-braking halt on second and the door
opened, let them out into the narrow maze, the windowless
windings of stairs and passages, granite which seeped water
squeezed out of the stones by the vast mass above their
heads.

And music—music played here constantly, echoing madly
through the deep stone halls. There was other music too, conduits, which came up from the rivers, and these sang softly
when the hand touched them, with the force of the water
surging in them up or down. There were power conduits,
shielded and painted; there were areas posted with yellow signs
and DANGER and KEEP OUT, subterranean mysteries which
were the business of the Deep Builders, and not for liners,
and never for the soft-handed Residents of the high tower
who came slumming here, thrill-seeking.

"Going my way?" Sarah asked of Sam, and off they went,
by the stairs to the next level down, to the ancient Worm; but
Johnny hugged Poll against him and took the corridor that
snaked its way with one of the waterpipes, toward the core of
second level; the Pillar was liner even to its decor, which was
old tackle and scrawled signatures . . . they walked in
through an arch that distinguished itself only by louder
music—one had to know where one was down at the Bottom,
or have a guide, and pay; and no Residents got shown to the
Pillar, or to the Worm, not on the guides' lives. He found his
favored table; next the big support that gave the place its
name, around which the tables wound, a curve which gave
privacy, and, within the heartbeat throb of the music, calm
and warmth after the shrieking winds.

He and Poll ordered dinner from the boy who did the
waiting; a tiny-"tiny," he said, measuring a span with his fin-

gers—glass of brew, because they were going out on the lines again tomorrow, and they needed their heads unswollen.

They had of course other pleasures in mind, because there was more to the Pillar than this smoky, music-pulsing den, and the food and drink; there were the rooms below, down the stairs beyond, for such rest as they had deserved.

He finished his good meal, and Poll did, and they sat there sipping their brew and eyeing one another with the anticipation of long acquaintance, but the brew was good too, and what they had been waiting for all day, with the world swinging under their feet and exertion sucking the juices out of them. They were that, old friends, and it could wait on the drink, slow love, and slow quiet sleep in the Bottom, with all the comforting weight of the City on their backs, where the world was solid and warm.

"Tallfeather."

He looked about, in the music and the smoke. No one used his last name, not among the highliners; but it was not a voice he knew . . . a thin man in Builders' blue coveralls and without a Builders' drawling accent either.

"Tallfeather, I'd like to talk with you. Privately."

He frowned, looked at Poll, who looked worried, tilted his head to one side. "Rude man, that."

"Mr. Tallfeather."

No one said Mister in the Bottom. That intrigued him. "Poll, you mind? This man doesn't get much of my time."

"I'll leave," Poll said. There was a shadow in Poll's eyes, the least hint of fear, he would have said, but there was no cause of it that he could reckon.

"No matter," the man said, hooking his arm to pull him up. "We've a place to go."

"No." He rose to his feet all right, and planted them, glared up at the man's face. Shook his arm free. "You're begging trouble. What's your name? Let me see your card."

The man reached for his pocket and took one out. *Manley,* it said, *Joseph,* and identified him as an East Face Builder, and that was a lie, with that accent. Company number 687. Private employ.

So money was behind this, that could get false cards. He looked for Poll's opinion, but she had slipped away, and he was alone with this man. He sat down at the table again, pointed to the other chair. "I'd be crazy to walk out of here with you. You sit down there and talk sense or I do some talking to security, and I don't think you'd like that, would you?"

Manley sat down, held out his hand for the card. Johnny gave it to him. "So who are you?" Johnny prodded.

There was no one, at the moment, near them. The huge pillar cut them off from sight and sound of others, and the serving boy was gone into the kitchen or round the bend.

"You're of the 48 East," Manley said, "and this project you're on . . . you know what kind of money that throws around. You want to stay on the lines all your life, Tallfeather, or do you think about old age?".

"I don't mind the lines," he said. "That's what I do."

"It's worth your while to come with me. Not far. No tricks. I have a friend of yours will confirm what I say. You'll trust him."

"What friend?"

"Jino Brown."

That disturbed him. Jino. Jino involved with something that had to sneak about like this. Jino had money troubles. Gambled. This was something else again. "Got a witness of my own, remember? My teammate's going to know who you are, just in case you have ideas."

"Oh, she does know me, Mr. Tallfeather."

That shook his confidence further, because he had known Poll all his life, and Poll was honest.

And scared.

"All right. Suppose we take that walk."

"Good," Manley said, and got to his feet. Johnny rose and walked with him to the door, caught the young waiter before he went out it. "Tommy, lad, I'm going with Mr. Manley here." He took the order sheet from the boy's pocket and wrote the name down and the company number, probably false. "And you comp my bill and put your tip on it, and you remember who I left with, all right?"

"Right," the boy said. Builder by birth, Tommy Pratt, but small and unhealthy and sadly pale. "You in some kind of trouble, Johnny?"

"Just remember the name and drop it in the liners' ears if I don't come back before morning; otherwise forget it."

"Yes, sir."

Manley was not pleased. Johnny smiled a taut, hard smile and walked with him then, out the winding ways where the man wanted to lead him. In fact it was curiosity and nerves that brought him with Manley, an ugly kind of curiosity. He was no Resident to go rubber-kneed at the sight of the lines, but this had something to do with those he was going out there with, and where their minds were, and this he wanted to know.

There was another dive a good distance beyond, down a series of windings and up and down stairs, on the very margin of the territory he knew in the Bottom; and being that close to lost made him nervous too.

But Jino was there, at the table nearest the door, stood up to meet him, but did not take him back to the table; walked him with his hand on his shoulder, back into one of the rooms most of these places had, where the pounding music and the maze gave privacy for anything.

"What is this?" Johnny asked, trusting no one now; but Jino urged him toward a chair at the round table that occupied this place, that was likely for gambling—Jino *would* know such places. Manley had sat down there as if he owned the place, and stared at both of them as they sat down. "I'll tell you what it is," Manley said. "There's a flaw on the East Face 90th, you understand?"

"There's not a flaw."

"Big one," said Manley. "Going to deviate the whole project a degree over."

"Going to miss some important property," Jino said, "whatever the computers projected. *We're* the ones go out there; the computers don't. We say."

He looked at Jino, getting the whole drift of it and not at all liking it.

"Mr. Tallfeather," Manley said. "Property rides on this. *Big* money. And it gets spread around. There is, you see, a company that needs some help; that's going to be hurt bad by things the way they're going; and maybe some other companies have an in with the comp operators, eh? Maybe this just balances the books. You understand that?"

"What company? That ATELCORP thing that made the fuss?"

"You don't need to know names, Mr. Tallfeather. Just play along with the rest of your team. They'll all be in on it. All. And all it takes is your cooperative—silence."

"Sure, and maybe you're telling that to all of them, that I went with it."

Manley frowned deeply. "You're the last holdout, Tall-

feather, you and your sister. You two are the sticking point,
the ones we knew would have been hard to convince. But it's
a team play. You respect that. You don't want to cut your
three partners out of that company's gratitude. Think of your
old age, Tallfeather. Think how it is when you stop being
young, when you still have to go out there. And this company's gratitude—can go a long way."

"Money," Jino said. "Enough to set us up. Influence. We're
set, you understand that, Johnny? It's not crooked; just what
he said, balancing the influence the others have on the com-
puter input. So both sides are bought. This goes *high*, Johnny;
the Council, the companies they run . . . this is a power
grab."

"Mr. Brown," Manley cautioned.

"Johnny's reasonable. It's a matter of explaining."

"I think I see it," Johnny said in a flat voice.

"Trust the company," Manley said. "Someone's talking to
your sister too."

Panic settled over him. He settled back in his chair. He
went out on the lines with these people. Had to. It was all he
had. "Sarah will go with it if I do. Who's financing this?
What company? If we're in it, I figure we should know."

"Never mind that."

"Just shut up and take it," Jino said. "And agree with the
charts. I do that part of it. You just keep your mouth shut
and take your cut."

"All right," he said. "All right. No problem from me." He
pushed back from the table. "I'd better get back, you mind? I
left some instructions if I didn't get back quick."

Jino frowned and motioned him gone. He gathered himself
up, walked out, through the main room and down the corridors, with an increasingly leaden feeling at his gut.

Tommy's face lit with relief to see him; he clapped the boy
on the shoulder. "Poll?" he asked, and Tommy blinked and
looked about.

"I think she left," Tommy said.

He checked. She was not in the room they had rented. Not
upstairs. He frowned and left, hunting Sarah, down in the
Worm.

She was gone too. So was Sam Kenny.

He sat down, ordered a drink to occupy a table by the
door of the Worm, a den as dark and loud and smoky as the
Pillar, but smaller and older; and he asked a few questions,

but not too many, not enough to raise brows either among
the liners there or with the management. The drink gradually
disappeared. He sat with a sick feeling at his stomach and ordered another.

Finally she came in. He restrained himself from jumping
up, sat cool and silent while Sarah spotted him and walked
over with a distressed look that told where she had been. She
pulled up another chair and sat down.

"I know," he said. "They got to you and Sam?"

"What do we do, Johnny?"

"What did you tell them we'd do?"

"I told them we'd think about it."

"I told them we'd go with it," he said. "What do you think
we are, Sarah?"

Her shoulders fell and she sat and looked morose. His
drink came and he pushed it over to her, ordered one for
himself. "I don't think," she said when they were alone, "I
don't think they trust us, Johnny, whatever they promise."

He thought about that, and it frightened him, agreeing
with his own thought. "We go along with it. It's all we can
do. Report it . . . we don't know what it would stir up, or
how high; or what enemies we'd have."

She nodded.

They took rooms in the Worm. He took a bottle with him,
and Sarah did, and he at least slept. Sam never did come back,
to his knowledge.

And came late morning, he and Sarah walked together to
the service lift, got on it with two other liners not of their
team who were making the ride up to tenth; they exchanged
no words. The other liners got off, and they said nothing to
each other, the whole long ride to the ninetieth.

Down the carpeted hall to the access hall: they were first
to arrive. They stripped and put on the suits, waited around
with hoods back and gloves off. Sam showed up, and Poll,
avoiding their eyes. There was poison in the air. There had
never been that, quarrels yes, but not this. Jino showed, clipboard in hand, and the silence continued. "Blast you," Jino
said. "Look up, look alive. Get your minds on it. Who's been
talking?"

Johnny shook his head. Jino looked from one to the other
of them. "What's wrong?" Johnny asked. "Jino, maybe we
and you better get this all straight. Or maybe we don't go out
there today."

"Questions, that's all." Jino took his suit and harness off the hook and started stripping like the rest of them. "Had the man back, you understand me? Stopped me, asking . . . asking whether any of the team might have had second thoughts. Any of you been talking?"

Heads shook, one by one.

"Right then." Jino climbed into the suit, zipped up, and the rest of them starting getting hoods up and masks hung in place. "It's all right," Jino said. He belted the harness about his chest and up through his legs, took the clipboard and hung it from his belt. "It's started, anyway. I've got the figures. All we have to do is keep developing this data; and it's all figured; they gave it to me the way we have to turn it in. Is that hard?"

They shook their heads again. There was a bitter taste in Johnny's mouth. He shrugged into his own harness, pulled it up, hooked it, checked the precious line, coiled in its case, to be sure it rolled and that the brake held as it should.

"So get moving," Jino said. "Go, get out there."

They moved. Sam opened the access door, a round hatch; and wind howled in, nothing to what it would do if the back door were open. Poll swore and bounced slightly, nervousness; it was always this way, going out. Sam went first, hooked his first line to the access eye, eased out of sight, bowed in the wind, facing outward for a moment and then turning to face the building. Sarah moved up next, as soon as that eye was free.

His turn. He hooked on, looked out into the blasting wind, at the view Residents never saw unshielded. He pulled his tinted mask down, and the sunglare resolved itself into the far dizzying horizon. He stepped to the ledge, jerked to be sure the brake was holding on his line before he trusted his weight to it. This was the part the groundlings could never take, that first trusting move in which he swung out with all the dizzy curve of the city-mountain at his feet, windows and ledges . . . shielded ledges below, as the curve increased, and finally mere glass tiles, thick and solid, the windows of the Bottom, which were skylights, thick because there was always the chance of getting something dropped through one . . . winter ice, which built up and crashed like spears weighing hundreds of pounds; or the falling body of a liner, which had happened; or something a liner dropped, which was enough

to send a man to the Bottom for a month: even a bolt
dropped from these heights became a deadly missile.

Ninety floors down.

The insulated suits protected from the cold, barely. The
masks did, or the windchill would have frozen their eyes and
membranes and robbed them of breath; every inch of their
bodies was covered. He clipped his line to another bolt and
let the last retract, dropping and traversing in a wide arc that
made all the stones blur past, caught the most convenient
ledge with a practiced reach that disdained the novice's
straightline drop and laborious climb back; he had his line of
ascent above him now, the number ten; Sarah had the elev-
enth; Sam the twelfth; Poll, coming after him, number nine;
Jino number eight, near the access. Climb and map and
watch for cracks, real ones, which was their proper job; and
swear to a lie. He tried not to think of that. They still had a
job to do, the routine that kept the building in repair; and out
here at least, the air was clean and minds had one steady job
to occupy all their attention—one small move after another,
eyes straight ahead and wits about them.

They checked and climbed, steady work now, feet braced,
backs leaning against the harness. They had come out after
the sun was well up; paused often for rests. He felt the day's
heat increasing on his back, felt the trickle of sweat down his
sides. The ice was burned off, at least. None of that to make
feet slip and line slip its brake in slides that could stop even a
liner's heart. His mask kept the air warm and defogged itself
immaculately, a breathing that those who spent their lives in
the City never experienced, sharp and cold and cleansing. He
got near the windows as the day wore on toward afternoon.
He could see his own monstrous reflection in the tinted glass
he passed, like some black spider with a blank, reflective face;
and dimly, dimly, the interiors of the offices of ATELCORP: he
recognized the logo.

He was out of love with them. But a woman at the desk
nearest the glass looked up at him with bright innocent eyes.
She smiled; he smiled, uselessly, behind his mask—freed a
hand and waved, and watched her reaction, which looked like
a gasp. He grinned, let go the other and then, businesslike,
reached for the next clip and edged higher, to spider over a
bit onto the blank wall. But the woman mouthed him something. He motioned with his hand and she said it again. He
lipread, like many a liner, used to the high winds, the same as

they used handsigns. He mimed a laugh, slapped his hand on
his gut. Her half-mirrored face took on a little shock. She
laughed then. The invitation had been coarse.

He let go again, mimed writing with his hand, teasing her
for her number. She laughed and shook her head, and he
reckoned it time to move on.

He had fallen behind. Poll and Sam and Sarah were ahead,
two floors above, Jino about even with him. He made a little
haste on the blank wall, like them, where there were no windows to be careful of, reach and clip, adjust the feet, reach
and clip, never quite loose. They reached the ledge of the
hundred, and stopped for a breather, eyed the clouds that had
come in on the east, beyond the ringlet of other towers. "Going to have to call it soon," Sam said.

"We just move it over," Jino said. "Traverse five over,
work it down, come back to the 90 access."

They nodded. That was what they wanted, no long one
with that moving in. It boded ice.

And when they had worked the kinks from backs and
shoulders and legs, they lined along the ledge, the easy way,
and dropped into their new tracks, a windowless area and
quick going. Johnny leaned over and bounced as he hit the
wall, started working downward with enthusiasm. It faded.
Muscles tired. He looked up, where Sam and Sarah seemed
occupied about some charting; so maybe they had found
something, or they were doing a little of the minor repair
they could do on the spot.

It was a good route up; the computers were right, and it
was the best place. He looked down between his feet at the
hazy Bottom, where the ground prep had already been done
with so much labor, tried not to let his mind dwell on the lie.
It was getting toward the hour they should come in anyway,
and the wind was picking up, shadows going the other way
now, making the tower a little treacherous if he kept looking
down, a dizzying prospect even to one accustomed to it.

Wind hit; he felt the cold and the lift carried him almost
loose from his footing.

Suddenly something dark plummeted past. He flinched and
fell inward against the stone, instinct. Something dropped—
but big; it had been. . . . He looked up in the shadow,
squinted against the flaring sky, saw the channel next to him
vacant; Sarah's channel, a broken line flying.

He flung himself outward with his legs, looked down, but

she had fallen all the way by now, spun down the long slow
fall.

Sarah.

It hit him then, the grief, the loss. He hung there against
the harness. By now the rest of the team had stopped, frozen
in their places. He stayed put, in the windy silence, and the
belt cutting into his back and hips, his legs numb and braced.

His hands were on his lines. He caressed the clip that was
between him and such a fall, and was aware of a shadow, of
someone traversing over to him.

Poll. She hung there on her lines' extension, touched his
shoulder, shook at him and pointed up and over. Shouted in
the wind and the muffling of the mask. *Access*, he lipread.
Get to the access.

He began, the automatic series of moves that were so easy,
so thoughtless, because the equipment held, but Sarah's had
not. Sarah was down there, his own flesh and bone spattered
over all the protected skylights on the mountain's long, slow
curve.

He began shaking. He hung there against the flat stone, out
in the wind, and his legs started shaking so that he could not
make the next step, and hands froze so that he could not
make the next release, could not make the swing across to the
next track, suspended over that.

Another came. Sam, and Poll. He felt them more than
saw, bodies hurtling near him on their lines, and he hung
there, clinging with his fingers, flinched, shuddering as a third
plummeted and came against him from the back, spider fashion.

They lined to him. He knew what they were doing and
would do, but he was frozen, teeth chattering. The cold had
gotten to him, and he clung desperately to the wall, trying to
see nothing else, felt them hooking to him, felt them release
his lines.

He screamed, hurled free by the wind, swung down and
stopped against the lines as they jerked taut against his body
harness. He hung there, swinging free in the wind gusts, while
the twilit city spun and flared in streaks and spirals before his
blurring eyes. He heard a scream, a chorus of them, and
there was another body plummeting past him, an impact that
hit his shoulder and spun him. He tried to catch it, but the
body got past him as he spun, and he watched, watched
downward as it spread itself like a star on the winds and

whirled away, in slow, terrible falling. Vanished in perspective. He never saw it hit. Tried to convince his mind to see it soar away, safe, unharmed; but it had hit; and it was a terrible way to die. Like Sarah.

His stomach heaved. He swayed in the buffets of the wind. Two of their team fallen. *Two.* He hung there, thinking of the line, that never gave, never; it was beyond thought that it should give. But two had, and he hung there with his body flying loose from the building in the gusts.

He twisted his head, tried to help himself, but his arms were too chilled to move accurately and his hands fumbled in trying to turn himself against the stone. He managed to look up, saw the two other survivors of the team working at the latch of the access three stories above. They would winch him in, once safe themselves. But it was not opening.

Jammed. Locked. Someone had locked them out here.

And two of their lines had broken.

He moved again as a gust of wind caught him, slammed him against the building. The impact numbed that arm. He manipulated the extension hook with the right arm, shot it out, and even when the wind swayed him farthest that way, it was short of the next hook. He retracted it finally, let it swing from its cord again and his aching arm fall as he sank in his harness. He struggled to lift his head finally, saw his teammates likewise still. Their lines had tangled. They were in trouble, twisted in the wind, exhausted. Now and again when he would look up one of them would be striking at the hatch, but there was no sound; the wind swallowed it. There were no windows where they were, in this blind recess. No one saw; no one heard.

The light waned, wrapped in advancing cloud in a streaming of last colors. The wind kept blowing, and mist began to spit at them, icing lines, icing the suits, chilling to the bone. He watched the lights come on in the far, far tower of Queens, thinking that perhaps someone might be looking out, that someone might see a skein of figures, that someone might grow curious, make a call.

No. There was no way they could see so far. He could unclip, die early. That was all.

He did not. He hung there with his body growing number, and the chill working into his bones. How many hours until someone missed them? Until the other liners started asking questions?

He looked up, immense effort, saw what looked like the lift of an arm to the hatch in the dusk. They were still trying. "Who fell?" he tried to ask. He could not; waved a feeble hand to let them know he was alive. In the masks, in the dark suits, there was no seeing who it was in that tangle of line and bodies.

It darkened further into night, and he felt ice building up on his right side, flexed and cracked it off his suit. The harness about his chest and waist and groin was stressed at an angle, gravity and the buffeting of the wind cutting off the blood to one side. He struggled, and began, when the wind would sway him far out and then slam him back against the building, to think of the thin line fraying with every move. It was not supposed to.

Was not supposed to. They had been murdered.

Were dying out here because of it.

Out and back. He moaned from the pain, a numb whimper, having had enough, and having no one to tell it to. Again . . . out and against the wall.

It went on and on, and the clouds cut off even the stars from view, leaving just the city lights, that streaked and spun and danced like jewels. He got a sliver of ice in his fingers, slipped it under his mask and into his mouth to relieve the thirst that tormented him; his arm dropped like lead. He stopped moving, aware only of the shriek of the wind, of battering like being taken up by a giant and slammed down again.

Release the catch, a tiny voice whispered to him. *Give up. Let go.*

Someone did. A body hurtled past, a thin, protesting cry—mind changed, perhaps? Grief? Outrage?

He could not see it fall. It went into the dark and the distance, a shadow for a moment against the light below, and then gone, kited on the winds.

Don't they find us down there? he wondered. *Don't they know?* But all the Bottom down there was shielded over for construction. No one would know, unless someone looked out at the moment of falling, unless someone just chanced to see.

There was one of his team left up there. One companion in the dark. "Who are you?" he cried. "Who?"

His voice was lost. No answer came to him.

He sank against the harness, let his head fall, exhausted, senses ebbing.

Came to again at the apex of a swing, screamed as he hung free a moment; but he was still lined. The jerk came, and he slammed against the stone, sobbed with the battering. The night was black, and the corner where they were was black. He dangled and twisted, his lines long since fouled, saw the whole world black, just a few lights showing in the Bottom, the tower of Queens a black, upsweeping point of darkness.

Early morning? How many hours until daylight?

"Who's still up there?" he called in a lull in the wind.

No answer. He dropped his head to his chest, tautened his muscles as a random gust got between him and the building, flying him almost at a right angle to the building, so that the city and the sky spun dizzyingly. The gust stopped. He swung back, hit, went limp, knowing the next such might break his back.

Let it go, the inner voice urged him. *Stop the pain.*

The line might break soon. Might save him the effort. Surely his harness had been tampered with like all the others, while it hung there in the access room.

Jino, he thought, Jino, who had stayed nearest the access. But the door had jammed.

Get rid of this team, get another one assigned more compatible with someone's interests.

He thought about that. Thought about it while the wind slammed and spun at him and the cold sank deeper.

Light flared above. He tried to look up, saw the hatch open, black figures in it against the light. A beam played down, caught him in the face.

The line slipped. He went hot and cold all over at that sickening drop. He twisted, tried to lift an arm, raised it a little. The light centered on him. The wind caught him, a brutal slam out and across the beam. And then the light moved off him. He shouted, hoarse and helpless. Then he felt one of the lines begin to shorten, pulling him in. The winch inside the access; they had that on it, a steady pull, dragging the line over the stone, one line, up and up. He hung still, hardly daring breathe, more frightened now than before . . . to live through this, and to have the line break at the last moment. . . . The wind kept catching him and swinging him far out so that he could see the lights below him.

Almost there. He twisted to see. Hands plucked at the taut line, seized his collar, his shoulders, his chest harness, dragged him backward over the sill of the access. One last sinking into human hands, an embrace which let his cold body to the floor, faces which ringed about him. Someone pulled his mask off, and he flinched at the white light.

"Alive," that one said. Liners. The hatchway was still open. He tried to move, rolled over, looked and saw his teammate, first recovered on the tangled lines, lying on the floor by him, open-eyed and dead.

Jino. It was Jino. He lay there, staring at the dead face. Jino tampered with the harness . . . maybe; or someone else—who locked the door and left them all out there . . . to die.

"There's no more," he heard someone shout; and the hatch boomed shut, mercifully cutting off the wind. His rescuers lifted his head, unzipped the tight suit. "Harness," he said. "Someone tampered with the lines." They were brothers. They had to know.

"Lock that door," one of them said. He let his breath go then, and let them strip the suit off him, winced as one of them brought wet towels that were probably only cold water; it felt scalding. He lived. He lay and shivered, with the floor under him and not the empty air and the dark. Someone seized his face between burning hands while continuing to soak the rest of his body. Dan Hardesty: he knew the team, four men and a woman; the 50 East. "What do you mean, tampered? What happened?"

"Tried to fake the reports," he said. "Someone wanted the reports doctored, and didn't trust us. They killed us. They—or the other side. Tampered with the harness. Lines broke. *Two lines broke out there.*"

They hovered about him, listening, grim-faced. His mind began to work with horrid clarity, two and two together; it took more than one team bought off. Took buying all that worked this section; them too. The 50th. He lay there, shivering as the water started to cool, thinking ugly thoughts, how easy it was to drop a body back out there.

"Someone," he said, "jammed the latch. Locked us out there."

Dan Hardesty stared at him. Finally scowled, looked above him at one of his own, looked down again. "Bring that water up to warm," he said. "Move it. We've got to get him out of here."

He shivered convulsively, stomach knotting up, limbs jerking; they set him up. They got the warmer cloths on him and he flinched, tried to control his limbs. His left leg and his right were blackening on the sides; his left arm already black. "Look at his back," the woman Maggie said, and he reckoned it was good he could not see it. They sponged at it, trying to get him back to room temperature.

"Tommy Pratt got worried," Dan said. "Started asking questions—where were you, what was going on—other questions got asked. So we figured to come up to your site and check. Wish we'd come sooner, Johnny. Wish we had."

He nodded, squeezed his eyes shut, remembering his friends. Sarah. Part of him. It was not grief, for Sarah. It was being cut in half.

Someone pounded at the door. "Security," someone called from outside.

"Hang Tommy," Dan said.

They were unlocking the door. "Help me up," he begged of them; and they did, held him on his feet, wrapped one of the towels about him. The door opened, and security was there, with drawn guns.

"Got an accident," Dan said. "Team went out, lines fouled, wind broke them. We got two in; one live, one dead; the others dropped."

"Call the meds," the officer in charge said. Johnny shook his head, panicked; the hospital—corporation-financed. He did not want to put himself in their hands.

"I'm not going," he said, while the call went out. "Going to the Bottom. Get myself a drink. That's what I want. That's all I want."

The officer pulled out a recorder. "You up to making a statement, Mr.—"

"Tallfeather. Johnny." His voice broke, abused by the cold, by fright. He leaned against the men holding him up. "I'll make your statement. We were out on the 90s, going down. My sister Sarah . . . her line broke. The others tried to spider me down, to come back, and the lines fouled. Hours out there. Lines broke, or maybe one suicided. The wind—"

"Man would," Dan said. "You ever been Outside, officer?"

"Names. ID's."

Dan handed his over. Another searched Johnny's out of his coveralls, turned everyone's over, dead and living. The officer read them off into the recorder. Returned them, to the living. "Dead man here?"

"Team boss," Johnny said, moistening his lips. "Jino Brown. The others dropped."

The officer looked at Dan Hardesty and his team. "Your part in this?"

"Friends. They didn't show and we came checking. Boy named Tommy Pratt in the Pillar, he put us onto it. Let the man go, Mister. He's had enough."

The officer bent down and checked Jino's corpse, touched the skin, flexed the fingers.

"Frosted," Dan said. "Pulled his mask off, you understand? No mask out there, you die quick. Painless, for those afraid of falling."

"Thought liners weren't afraid of falling."

"Lot of us are," Dan said levelly. "Come on, officer, this man's *sister* died out there."

"Think he'd be more upset about it, wouldn't you?"

Johnny swung; they stopped him, and the officer stepped back a pace.

"All right," the officer said carefully. "All right, all right. Easy."

Johnny sucked air, leaned there, glaring at the officer, cooled his mind slowly, thinking of what he wanted—to be out, down, away from them—alive.

The officer thumbed his mike. "Got an accident here," he said. "Liners fouled, one survivor, Tallfeather, John Ames, city employee."

Noise came back. The officer touched the plug in his ear and his eyes flickered, looking at them. The door opened, the rest of the security officers showing two meds in. "Get him out," the officer said with a gesture at Jino's body. "The other one says he's walking."

The meds ignored the body, turned on him. Johnny shook them off, shook his head while one of them told him about massive contusions and blood clots and his brain. "Get me my clothes," he told the liners. One did.

"Somebody," Dan was saying, "needs to go out there and get those bodies in off the Bottom."

He heard. Maybe he should protest, give way to grief, insist to be one to go even if there was no chance of his walking that far. He had no interest in finding Sarah's body, or Poll's, or Sam's. He had only one interest, and that was to get his clothes on, to get out of here. He managed it, wincing, while the meds conferred with the police and wondered if there were not some way to arrest him to get him to the hospital.

"Get out of here," Dan warned them. There was sullen silence.

"Mr. Tallfeather," one of the medics appealed to him.

He shook his head. It hurt. He stared hatefully at them, and they devoted their attention to Jino, who was beyond protest.

"Free to go?" Dan asked the police.

"We've got your numbers," the officer said.

Dan said nothing. Johnny walked for the door between two of them, trying not to let his knees give under him.

They got him to the service lift, got a better grip on him once inside, because he gave way when the car dropped, and he came near to fainting. They went down, down as far as they would go, got out in the passages, walked the way to the Worm.

He fainted. He woke up in a bed with no recollection of how he had gotten there; and then he did remember, and lay staring at the ceiling. An old woman waited on him, fed him; labored over him. Others came in to look at him, liners and Builders both. When he was conscious and could get his legs under him he tottered out into the Worm itself and sat down and had the drink he had promised himself, remembering Sarah, who had sat with him—over there. And the word whispered through the Worm that there was a strike on, that none of the liners were going out; that there was a Builder slowdown, and the name of Manley and ATELCORP was mentioned.

There was a quiet about the place, that day, the next. There were police, who came and took photographs inside the Worm and read a court order in dead silence, ordering the Builders back to work. But the silence hung there, and the police were very quiet and left, because no one wanted to go Outside but liners and the whole City would die if the Builders shut things down. Up in the towers they knew their computers. A lot was automated; a lot was not. The computers were all their knowledge.

There was talk of an investigation. The Mayor came on vid and appealed for calm; said there was an investigation proceeding about gang activity, about bribes; about corruption in certain echelons far down the corporation lists. There was a lot of talk. It all moved very quickly.

"We'll get something," Dan Hardesty told him. "We got the one that went by Manley. Fellow named George Bettin. ATELCORP's man. Flunky; but we got him."

"They'll hang him out," he said quietly, hollowly. "So much for Manley. Yes. We got him."

And that day the Bettin trial started he rode the lift up to the hundredth, and walked to one of the observation windows, but when he got close to it, with the far blue distance and the Newark spire rising in his view, he stopped.

It was a long time before a passerby happened to see him there, against the wall; before a woman took him by the arm and coaxed him away from the wall, down the corridor. They called the meds; and they offered him sedatives.

He took them. Rode the lift down. That itself was terror. He had had dreams at night; wakened with the world hanging under him and the sky above and screamed until the Worm echoed with it.

The drugs stopped that. But he stayed below, refused to go near the windows. Three, four days, while the Manley/Bettin trial dragged on. They never called him to testify; never called any of the liners.

But a message came to the Worm, signed with big names in ATELCORP; and that failed to surprise him. He went, up the far, far distance to the nineties.

He walked in, looked about him, flinched from the windows, a mere turning of his head. They wanted him to go into an office with windows. Paul Mason, the door said, President.

"Mr. Tallfeather," someone said, trying to coax him. He turned his back to the windows.

"He comes out here," he said, staring at the blank wall in front of him, the fancy wallpaper, the civic contribution citations. "He comes out to *me*."

He stood there. Eventually someone came, and a hand rested on his shoulder. "The windows. I understand, Mr. Tallfeather. I'm terribly sorry. Paul Mason. I called you here. You want to walk back this way, please?"

He walked, trembling, until they were in the hallway, in the safe, stone-veneer hall, and Mason drew him into a small windowless office, a desk, a few bookshelves, some chairs, immaculate, expensive. "Sit down," Mason urged him. "Sit down, Mr. Tallfeather."

He did so, sank into a chair. A secretary scurried in with an offer of hot tea.

"No," Johnny said quietly.

"Please," Mason said. "Something else."

"Tea;" he said. The secretary left in haste. Mason sat in another chair, staring at him . . . a thin man, white-haired, with hard lines.

"Mr. Tallfeather," Mason said. "I've been briefed on your case. My staff came across with it. I've heard what happened."

"Heard," he echoed. Maybe there was still a craziness in his eyes. Mason looked uneasy.

"It was a man of ours, George Bettin. That's as far as it went; you've followed the trial."

He nodded, staring at Mason all the while.

"ATELCORP has no legal liability—certainly no criminal fault—but we want to make amends for this. To do right by you."

"To get the liners working again," he said bitterly.

"That, too, Mr. Tallfeather. I think your case, more than the end of the trial—I think justice done on this level may do more to heal the breach. We want to offer you a position. This office. A job."

"Only I stop talking. I stop saying what happened."

"Mr. Tallfeather, the public welfare is at stake. You understand that; it's more than the project. The strike . . . is illegal. We can't have that."

He sat still a moment. "Yes, sir," he said, very, very softly. Wiped at his face. He looked about him. "Thoughtful of you. No windows."

"We're terribly sorry, Mr. Tallfeather. Our extreme condolences. Sincerely."

"Yes, sir."

"You just come to the office when you like. The door . . . doesn't go past the windows out there. You come when you like."

"Doing what, Mr. Mason?"

"We'll develop that."

"And I don't talk about my sister; about my team."

"We'd prefer not."

"You're scared," he said.

Mason's face went hard.

"I'll take the job," he said. The tea had just arrived. Mason put on a smile and rose, offered him a hand and clapped him on a still-bruised shoulder. "Your own secretary, you choose from the pool. Anything you want in the way of decor . . ."

"Yes, sir."

Mason smiled, which was not a smile. The secretary stood there with the tea, and stepped aside as Mason left. Johnny walked over and took the tray, set it down himself. "That's enough," he said. "Go away."

And that afternoon the press came, escorted by Mason.

"What do you think of the investigation, Mr. Tallfeather?"

"What was it like, Mr. Tallfeather?"

He gave it to them, all the titillation the vid addicts could ask for, how it felt, dangling in air like that, watching the others die. He was steady; he was heroic, quiet, tragic; appealed for the liners to go to work, for an end to the civic agony.

They left, satisfied; Mason was satisfied, smiled at him. Clapped him on the shoulder and offered him a drink. He took it, and sat while Mason tried to be affable. He was pleasant in turn. "Yes, Mr. Mason. Yes, sir."

He went back to his office, which had no work, and no duties.

He was back in the morning. Sat in his office and stared at the walls.

Listened to vid. The liners went back to work. The strike was over. The whole City complex breathed easier.

He stayed all the day, and left by his own door, when Mason left; used a liner's key to prep the service elevator; waited in the hall outside.

"Mr. Mason."

"Hello, Johnny."

He smiled, walked to join Mason, and Mason looked uncomfortable there in the hall, the quite lonely hall, in front of ATELCORP's big soundproof doors.

"Want you to come with me," he said to Mason.

"I'm sorry—" Mason started to say, headed for the doors.

Johnny whipped the hand and the razor from his pocket, encircled his neck, let it prick just a little. "Just want you to come with me," he said. "Don't yell."

Mason started to. The razor bit, Mason stopped, and yielded backward when he pulled him, down the hall, which at this time just before quitting time, with the Man in the hall—was very quiet.

"You're crazy," Mason said.

"Move." He jerked Mason backward, to the service elevator. Someone *had* come out. Saw. Darted back into the office. Mason started resisting and stopped at another nick.

"Look here," Mason gasped. "You're sick. It won't go bad for you; a hospital stay, a little rest . . . the company won't hold grudges; I won't. I understand—"

He dragged Mason backward into the lift; pushed TOP; and PRIORITY, with the key in. The door closed. The car shot up with a solid lift, that long, impossible climb. He let Mason loose, while he stood by the lift controls.

Mason stood against the wall and stared at him.

"I just want you," Johnny said ever so softly, "to go *with* me."

Mason's lips were trembling. He screamed aloud for help. It echoed in the small car.

"We have a head start," Johnny said. "Of course they'll come. But it takes the computers to override a service key. It'll take them a moment to realize that."

Mason stood and shivered. The car rose higher and higher, lurched at last to a stomach-wrenching stop. The door opened on a concrete room, and he took Mason by the arm and walked him outside the car. It left again. "I think they've called it," he said calmly. Used his left hand to pull the hatch lever.

The door slammed open, echoing; the wind hit them like a hammer blow, and Mason flinched. There was a wide balcony outside, heavy pipe from which lines were strung. Mason clung to the door and Johnny dragged him forward by the arm. All the world stretched about them in the twilight, and there was ice underfoot, a fine mist blowing, bitter cold, making muscles shake. Mason slipped, and Johnny caught his elbow, walked a step farther.

"I can't go out on the lines," Johnny said. "Can't look out the windows. But company helps. Doesn't it?" He walked him far out across the paving, his eyes on the horizon haze, and Mason came, shivering convulsively within the circle of his left arm. The wind hit them hard, staggered them both, made them slip a little on the ice. His right side was numb. He kept his arm about Mason, walked to the very railing. "No view like it, Mr. Mason. I dream of it. It's cold. And it's far. Look *down*, Mr. Mason."

Mason clutched at the railing, white-knuckled. Johnny let

him go, moved back from him, turned and walked back toward the lift doors.

The hatch opened. Police were there, with guns drawn. And they stayed within the doorway, leaned there, sickness in their eyes, hands clenched together on the levelled guns.

He laughed, noiseless in the wind, motioned toward the edge, toward Mason. None of the police moved. The world was naked about them. The soaring height of the other towers was nothing to this, to the City itself, the great Manhattan tower. He grinned at them, while the wind leached warmth from him.

"Go get him," he shouted at the police. "Go out and get him."

One tried, got a step out, froze and fell.

And slowly, carefully, holding up hands they could see as empty, he walked back to Mason, took his right hand and pried it from the icy rail; took the other, stared almost compassionately into a face which had become a frozen mask of horror, mouth wide and dried, eyes stark and wild. He put his arm about Mason like a brother, and slowly walked with him back to the police. "Mr. Mason," he said to them, "seems to have gotten himself out where he can't get back. But he'll be all right now." Mason's hands clung to him, and would not let go. He walked into the housing and into the lift with the police, still with his arm about Mason, and Mason clutched at him as the lift shot down. He smoothed Mason's hair as he had once smoothed Sarah's. "I had a sister," he said in Mason's ear. "But someone shut a door. On all of us. They'll convict Bettin, of course. And it'll all be forgotten. Won't it?"

The lift stopped at a lower floor. The police pushed him out, carefully because of Mason; and there were windows there, wide windows, and the twilight gleaming on the other buildings on the horizon. Mason sobbed and turned his face away, holding to him, but the police pulled them apart; and Mason held to the wall, clung there, his face averted from the glass.

"I don't think I want your job, Mr. Mason," Johnny said. "I'm going back out on the lines. I don't think I belong in your offices."

He started to leave. The police stopped him, twisted his arm.

"Do you really want *me* on trial?" he asked Mason. "Does the Mayor, or the Council?"

"Let him go," Mason said hoarsely. The police hesitated. *"Let him go."* They did. Johnny smiled.

"My lines won't break," he said. "There won't be any misunderstandings. No more jammed doors. I'll go back to the Bottom now. I'll talk where I choose. I'll talk to whom I choose. Or have me killed. And then be ready to go on killing. Dan Hardesty and the 50 East know where I am; and why; and you kill them and there'll be more and more to kill. And it'll all come apart, Mr. Mason, all the tower will come apart, the liners on strike; the Builders . . . no more cooling, no more water, no more power. Just dark. And no peace at all."

He turned. He walked back into the lift.

No one stopped him. He rode down through all the levels of the City, to the Bottom itself, and walked out into its crooked ways. Men and women stopped, turned curious eyes on him.

"That's Johnny Tallfeather," they whispered. "That's *him.*"

He walked where he chose.

There was peace, thin-stretched as a wire. The liners walked where they chose too; and the Builders; and the Residents stayed out of the lower levels. There was from all the upper floors a fearful hush.

So the city grew.

THE GENERAL

(Peking)

Man was old in this land. His dust was one with the dust which blew over the land, which had blown yellow and unstoppable from antiquity . . . which stained the great river and covered the land and settled again. The Forbidden City looked out on a land which moved, which shifted in this latter age of the world, beneath a lowering moon and the aging sun. Northward lay the vast ice sheet, but southern winds fended away that ancient enemy. Eastward lay the sea and southward the strangeness of the peninsulas and the isles; westward lay the plains, the endless plains, across which men and beasts moved again as they had moved in ages before . . . men wrapped and shielded against the sun, strange and shaggy as the beasts theey rode.

In the Forbidden City, life was abundant, sheltered by walls. There was beauty in the seasons, there was art from the cultivation of rare flowers to the intricate symbolism of gestures and nuances of dress; they had had time to grow elaborate and refined. The inhabitants named the city the City of Heaven and its beauty was beyond dreaming. It had soldiers . . . necessary when the impoverished plains tribes came with the winter winds, tribes which traded with them in good times, but which—rarely—turned, and beat themselves desperately and futilely against the walls.

The interior, which raiders never saw, was tranquility. Even the soldiers who defended the city were armed with beauty; weapons were works of art; and those were the only outward show permitted, for the walls were plain. The interior was beautiful as the accumulated treasure of ages could make it. Not all the beauty was of gold and jewels and jade, although there was a great deal of such work; but the quiet,

patient work of ordinary objects, a sense of place and per-
manence and above all of time . . . for while the City of
Heaven was not the oldest in the Earth, still it was conscious
of its passing years, and stored them up like treasures. It
loved its age. It found life good. It found no great ambition,
for it had been very long since its last outward motion; it
rested at the end of days. Its quality now was patience, and
meticulous loveliness, the contemplation of age and absorp-
tion in its private thoughts. Even the weather had been kind
in the years of younger memory, only lately turning drier.

Only the season finally came of the yellow wind, and the
dust, the worst dust of living memory.

Some whispered that it foretold a worse winter than any
living had seen.

Some whispered that it foretokened invasion, for the grass
must be dry and the hordes would move, and war among
themselves.

But a tribe tamer than the others came for the season's
trading and said, before departing again into the plains, that
in the years of green grass and little dust, the hordes had
multiplied, both man and beast; which meant greater numbers coming. And they told the City what the tribes had
known for years, that the City had known peace because the
hordes had massed for wars far to the west . . . that a single
horde had dominated all the others, and a leader had risen,
under whose horsetail banner all the hordes of the world-
plain moved. They themselves, said the more peaceful tribe,
prepared to go far away: so did all the friendly tribes, the
city's friends, who could not resist such a force. But the city
suspected otherwise, knowing that the tribes did not love
them. It was mere rumor, they said in council, some clever
trick to weaken their courage when these very peaceful tribes
ran out of trade goods and turned to brigandage.

But the dust storms grew worse, and the tribes did vanish.

The City of Heaven searched its records and its long
memory in more earnest. Indeed all these signs were con-
firmed, that one thing tended to lead to the other: they ought
to have mistrusted the green years and laid in greater store of
weapons.

Perhaps, some said now, they should call in the strangers
their children, who would come with their machines and their
starfarers' weapons and aid them to drive back the invaders.

But the citizens would not, because the strangers their children were rough-handed and sudden and liked to manage things their own way, which—again ancient experience of them forewarned—led to strangers seeing the beauties of the city; and seeing led to desiring; and desiring led to quarrelsome threats and to disturbances in the city. To call in the starfarers was to invite a horde far greater than that which might gather on the vast plains; and to invite plunder as grievous.

So they did not.

After all, the records indicated that many times in the eons past such intrusion had come, and the city, when well prepared and well led, had prevailed.

Only when the dust took on a stronger color in the west did they take clear alarm. This plume amid the blowing clouds was indeed broader than it had been in living memory and darker. It was their sole warning, with the tribes of the surrounding area gone: they were without eyes and ears now . . . but they were prepared in mind. The soldiers of the Forbidden City decorated their armor with ribbons, and polished their weapons and saw to their supplies of gunpowder . . . for more deadly weapons again involved the thankless and rowdy starfarers, and they would have none of it, as the enemy, they fully trusted, had no such arms. They filed out, great in number, footsoldiers, for the folk of the Forbidden City no longer traveled and preferred the stability of infantry in such few wars as they fought. They prepared to fight as they lived, with precision and elegance, ribbons streaming from armor and weapons and flowers decking their helms.

All the city turned out to see the soldiers on their way, waved gaily embroidered kerchiefs from the beautiful walls, danced dragons in the streets, threw flowers and cheered for the brave defenders of the city.

It was an event, not a crisis. Ah, they knew their danger, but the danger was remote, and their long tranquility behind their walls had made them philosophical and happy.

Nowhere near the whole of the city's young folk marched out. It was in fact only half, the Lion and Phoenix regiments, which went, those forces which this year's turn made active. The rest were spectators.

Such were Tao Hua and Kan Te, of the Dragon. Kan Te was a tall young son of the Guardian of the Morning Gate,

an excellent youth of straight limbs and a bright glance, and
a brave heart; and Tao Hua, as splendid a young woman as
Kan Te was a fine youth, daughter to renowed artists in inks.
They were soon to be married. All the world was good to
Tao Hua and Kan Te, and along with the rest of the cheering
city, they turned out in optimism, standing on the walls by
the western gate to wave cheer to their comrades and to take
in the spectacle. Their hearts lifted for the brave display. The
fighting was something beyond their imaginations, for while
they were soldiers, they had never fought in earnest. Usually
there were shots fired at a great distance and a few of the
barbarians would fall and that would be the end of the war.
It was all very tidy and none of the flower-decked armor was
sullied; in fact, in the last encounter, much before Tao Hua
and Kan Te were born, the army had come back with its
flowers unwilted, unstained and victorious.

There were drums and cymbals, and the dragon dancers
chained along at the army's side as they passed the gate.

"Perhaps we will be called up," said Tao Hua.

"Perhaps," said Kan Te, marking the size of the cloud; and
the least fear was in his heart, for he had heard his great-
grandfather talking with his grandparents and parents after
coming from council. "The council was divided about
whether to send more."

"Lion and Phoenix are very brave," said Tao Hua.

"They are not enough," said Kan Te, surer and surer of
this. He should not bear tales, things heard in family, but Tao
Hua bore them no further. He took her hand in his and they
watched the dust with the light of the dying sun piercing it
with strange colors. "Some wanted to defend the walls from
inside and some wanted to march out in all our strength; and
the result . . . the council sent only half, and left half behind. To send more, they said, would panic the people unnec-
essarily."

Tao Hua looked up at him, her face quite serene and
golden in the sun, and he thought again how he loved her.
He was afraid, perceiving a shaking in his world, as if it were
the tramp of hooves and feet, foretold in the dust.

"I dreamed," he said, further, "that all the grass of the
plains was gone; I dreamed that the Earth swarmed with men
and beasts and that they were much alike; I dreamed of tents
and campfires like stars across all the plain of the world; I

dreamed that the moon fell, and the moon was the hope of the city."

Tao Hua gazed at him, her black eyes reflecting the shifting clouds, and he thought again of the moon which fell, no bit comforted to have told his dream. There had always seemed time enough: the end of the world crept on at a leisurely pace, and in its ending there were beauties enough. There was no ambition left, but there was time . . . all the time human lives needed: it was only the Earth which had grown old. Love had not.

For the first time the thought of death came between them.

The column moved slowly, inexorable in its flow across the plain of the world, a flow which had begun years ago in the Tarim and surged to the western rim of the world-plain; which now flowed back again multiplied until the eye could not span its breadth, let alone its length.

The general rode at the head of the column: Yilan Baba, his men called him, Father Serpent, but snake he had been from his youth, cunning and deadly in his strike. Now he was very old, braced in the saddle with furs and the habit of years on horseback. It was an old pony that carried him, a beast he called Horse, which was one in a long succession of shaggy high-tempered beasts of similar bay color . . . how many, Yilan had forgotten; and this one had grown patient over the long traveling, and quiet of manner, tired, perhaps, as Yilan was tired, and old, as Yilan had gotten old . . . but that was not the complaint which gnawed at Yilan. He was thin beneath the quilted coats and leathers and furs, thin to the point of gauntness. His mustaches were grizzled; his braids were gray, his narrow eyes were lost in sun-wrinkles and his cheeks were seamed and hollowed by age and by the wasting disease which had come on him in this last year.

But if he looked, squinting, through the sun-colored dust which swirled about them, it seemed that he could see this place of his dreams, the Forbidden City, the City of Heaven. He imagined that he could see it, as he imagined it each dawning, when the sun rose out of the east and the colors streamed through the dusty wind. The wind out of the east breathed of green lands, of beauty, of wealth . . .

. . . of ending. A place to rest. Beyond, was only the sea.

"Give me the city," he had asked of the hordes which he had gathered. For all of a lifetime he had gathered them, he, Yilan, the Snake, from his mastery of his own tribe to mastery of all the tribes which rode the world-plain.

They came with tents and with wagons, with oxen and with swift horses and with patient feet, men and women and children of the hordes. With the drought on the plains he might have lost them, but he stirred them now with visions of final paradise, with a dream which he had prised from the lips of a man who had actually seen the City of Heaven.

He had gathered power all his life, which had been fifty-nine seasons, and which—he knew—would not be another. He wanted this thing, he wanted it—ah, beyond telling.

And the flesh grew thinner and the pain of his bones against the saddle grew all but unbearable; he bled from the saddlegalls, he was so thin, and his eyes watered so that much of the time he rode with the shame of tears on his cheeks.

"Drink, Yilan Baba," said a voice by his side. He looked into the young face of Shimshek, dark and fierce as a kite, who offered him kumiss and rode his pony close to Horse, so that he might steady him. He drank, and the liquor warmed him, but his hand was now so weak that he could not stopper the skin or long hold it. Shimshek caught it from him in time, and reached to grip his shoulder as they rode knee against knee. "Hold firm, Father, we will stop soon."

"The City will be in sight," he said, and comforted by the presence of his young lieutenant, he focused his mind and his eyes, and thought how long by now the plume of their dust might have been seen. "Hawk and Fox will go out with all others you can persuade," he said, his voice cracking; he steadied it and lifted his hand eastward, where he would send the forces. "And you must lead them. I no longer can, Shimshek."

"Father," Shimshek mourned. There was great sadness in his eyes, a genuine sorrow.

"I have taught you," said Yilan. Shimshek was not, in fact, his son; he had no son, though his wife's belly swelled with life. He loved this man as if he were a son, and trusted him with all that mattered. "Go," he said. "This time you lead."

Shimshek looked behind them, at the column of wagons which groaned after them, having in his eyes that look which was for the woman they both loved, and for things he could not say. There was fear in Shimshek's eyes that was not for the enemy, not for anything that he would yet name. Good, thought Yilan. Good, he knows; and yet Shimshek said nothing, because there was nothing which could be said. The task was for doing, and there was no help for it: he had himself fought his last battle, and knew it; and Horse knew it, who was also aging . . . by now Horse would have known the enemy, would have flared his nostrils and thrown his head and walked warily and eagerly with the scent of strangers and strange land coming on the winds. But he plodded, head hanging.

"Go," he said again, and Shimshek pressed his shoulder and then raced off full tilt, drumming his heels into his pony's side, shouting and kicking up the dust. "Hai ahi hai," he yelled, and the Wolf standard moved to Shimshek's summons, for Wolf was Shimshek's clan. Hawk and Fox moved when Yilan lifted his arm and waved those units foward; the warriors thundered past to the Wolf banner. More couriers went out on their swift ponies, rallying the others, a vast horde gathering to the command of Shimshek the Wolf in this the first skirmish of the campaign.

Another horseman rode to be near Yilan, dour and frowning, of Yilan's own years, but hale and powerful. Yilan envied him the power and the years yet left to him and looked him in the eyes. Boga was this one's name, gray and broad: *bull* was his name, and he had led all the hordes of the Danube.

Once.

"You send the Wolf . . . where?"

"To command." Again the hoarseness, which robbed his voice of the command it had once had. He was doubly grateful for the loyalty of Shimshek: his back would be cold indeed with Boga at it. "To *lead*, Boga. And your men will guard the column."

Hate burned in the old man's eyes, deep and vengeful. Yes, Yilan thought, and now even Shimshek fears this man. Advisedly, if yet without knowledge.

Boga rode away. Yilan watched the gathering of chiefs which instantly surrounded him. "Come on, Horse," he said, and thumped the bony sides and rode toward the group, rode among them, gaining guilty looks as he shouldered in. "Move," he said, "back to your troops," he ordered some;

and "Go with Shimshek," he ordered others. He commanded, and heads bowed and riders hurried off, and Boga was left to ride beside him. The gesture had tired him. He stared into the shifting light and the dust raised by Shimshek's swirling horsemen, and knew that hate was beside him.

"We camp in another degree of the sun," he said. He knew for a certainty what Shimshek had perhaps come to suspect in recent days, that he was dying quickly. That Boga wished the process hastened. "We have the city all but in sight," he said, to prod at Boga, for a perversity that he himself did not understand, except that in war, too, he had had such a habit, to draw the enemy out, and never to let him lie concealed.

"I did not believe you could do it, Yilan Baba. I did not, but you've proved me wrong."

Boga had resisted. He followed because his tribe could not hold apart from the other tribes; because he had commanded the Danube hordes and could still, if he went where they went. Inevitably in council there was Boga standing up and saying that the tribes must keep their independence each from the other. It sounded noble and traditional. It meant another thing; for the more he weakened, the more Boga had stopped saying such things. The more he began to die, the more a look was born in Boga's slitted eyes, like the look of a hungry beast.

"I know you," Yilan Baba said hoarsely.

"You should know me well by these many years, Father. We have had our differences, but indeed, have I not followed you?"

"I know you," Yilan said again, turning his head to look into Boga's eyes a second time; and this time something in Boga looked out of those eyes and seemed to go very cold. "We are old," said Yilan. "Very old, Boga. I know you."

The look became fear. Perhaps he should have feared in turn, but instead he smiled at Boga, and watched the fear grow, the certainty in Boga's mind that he was indeed known, and that the whispers which Boga whispered with others in the far places of the column were heard.

They rode side by side, he and his murderer, while Shimshek and much of the vanguard rode away to crush the forces which the city might send against them, which could not possibly stand against the might of all the tribes of the plain of the world.

His eyes wept, and this time not from the wind. He cherished a selfish hope that he might be able to see the city before he died. He did not speak of it in those terms, far from it. He acknowledged no weakness to Boga and his lot. He knew, in fact, that by challenging Boga he had just hastened the hour of his death. He should not have done it, perhaps, but he had commanded all his life, and he would not allow another to choose for him. Tonight then, likely tonight. Boga was thinking and planning and when Boga was sure then Boga would strike.

He thought of Gunesh riding behind him in the wagon, thought of her with the only pain he felt. Gunesh loved him; Shimshek did; and they were all the world. A baby grew in Gunesh's belly . . . not his son, but Shimshek's. He knew that. Of course he knew it. His health made other answers impossible. That even Shimshek and Gunesh betrayed him in this regard did not matter, because they were the two he loved best, and he could not wish better for her than she had for that young man, or he in her, or himself, in them. Sex had never been a matter of pride with him. It had never been, from his youth. He had gone through the motions, enjoyed a bawdy joke—but that part of his instincts was subordinated to his obsessions: not power, not precisely that—in fact, power bored him—hunger, perhaps, but he never wanted it sated. Nor was it vague or formless. He knew himself, ah, very well—and loved, and even hurt for the pain he caused, but he went on causing it.

Had prepared more of it, maneuvering Shimshek into command above Boga. But it was the right thing. Shimshek now had troops with him, tribe upon tribe . . . so it would be disaster for them to present Shimshek and the returning troops with the murdered body of Yilan Baba. Ah, no. They would do that only if they must.

He smiled to himself and stared into the dust with the wind cold on his cheeks, feeling the brush of Boga's knee against his as the ponies walked side by side, and the standard of the conquering hordes went before, the banner of the dying sun.

He still ruled, even making them kill him when he chose. That was always his power, that he chose everything he could, and gambled the rest.

And by the hour of camp the city appeared to them. A cry

went up from the column which stretched as far as the mind
could imagine. Ah, the tribes moaned. Ah, the women and
children said, and it was the sighing of the rumored sea, and
the rush of wind, and the breaking of thunder. *Ah*. The city
shimmered like a mirage, its roofs shone with gold and with
beauty in the light, and dust veiled it, which was the place of
Shimshek and the others, where battle raged. Yilan had no
doubt of the battle; had these not sufficed, he could have sent
more. They might crush the city with the wagons of women
and children alone, if they simply moved forward.

He wept, which he did continually, but it had meaning in
this moment; and in truth many of the warriors wept, and
waved their lances and raced their ponies. Here and there a
rider wasted precious gunpowder, which he did not repri-
mand, for after this there were no more battles for the horde,
because they should have conquered the whole of the known
world, and there was nothing more but the sea.

"Do we camp?" asked a young rider from Fox. He nodded
and looked at Boga. "Give the orders," he said. Boga rode off
to do so. The column halted, the wagons were unhitched, the
animals picketed. Yilan sat his horse and waited as he would
do every evening, until all was in order, until firepots were
brought from the wagons and cooking began.

The place of the wagon-tents was not chance; it was a matter of precedence. His own was central to the camp; and
those of his chieftains of the Hawk and Fox touching his
. . . but they were with Shimshek; and those of the Wolf
himself, but Shimshek was not there, and his underchiefs
were gone, so that there were only the families, wagons without defenders. Indeed, on his left was Boga's lynx standard,
and near it the standards of chiefs who had not gone with
Shimshek—all his enemies.

Boga's hour at last, Yilan thought to himself, riding slowly
into the trap, that harmless-looking area by his own wagon,
where Gunesh should be waiting. But there indeed Boga and
the others, who stood with their horses, dismounted, beside
the ladder of his wagon. He watched for blades, his heart
paining him for Gunesh, who might be dead; but no, not yet,
not until he should die. They would not dare, for fear of having all misfire. Cut off the snake's head before risking other
provocations. Boga was not stupid; thus, he was predictable.

It was a simple drink they gave him, a skin of kumiss, and
from Boga's own hand, while he was still in the saddle. He

looked at Boga, and there was a fearsome silence despite all
the noise and bustle of the camp . . . a silence and stark fear
in the faces all about that circle as he sat Horse with that
deadly gift in hand and looked from Boga to the rest of
them.

"I know you," he said again, and watched the hate in
Boga's eyes grow and the fear in the others' eyes increase.

He drank. He looked at them afterwards. Saw the fear no
whit abated. It was a different fear, perhaps, that of men who
suddenly felt transparent, and wondered if they had not
walked into some unnamed trap in which the stakes were not
quite as they had thought.

"Help me down," he said, and swung a leg over, used
Boga's arms to steady him, let Boga help him to the steps of
his wagon. Boga helped him up slowly, into the carpeted,
dark interior. "Light the lamps," he ordered, and Boga
uncovered the firepot and did so, a servant's duty; but Boga
let him exact this of him, enduring anything he might wish
. . . this night.

Then Yilan leaned back among the embroidered leather
cushions and rested his body on the carpets and the yellow
lamplight shone down on him. He shut his eyes and dreamed
of the city, and saw, from the slit of his eyes when he heard
a step departing, and felt the wagon quake, that Boga had
gone his way.

To lay traps and ambushes, doubtless.

O Shimshek, have a care!

"Husband?"

It was quite another step which came from behind the curtains, from the door by the forward chamber. A breath of
herbs came with her, a hint of sweetness unlike the dust and
the stink of urine that was the outside world. He opened his
eyes smiling, for Gunesh was by him, beautiful, brave
Gunesh, who had seen it all; there was terror in her eyes as
she knelt by him. He reached up and touched a gloved hand
to her cheek, for comfort.

"Will you eat, Yilan?"

He shook his head, made an effort to tug off his gloves.
She helped him; even that exertion tired him now. "I shall
smoke," he said. "And then I want you to go and pack a
little food, Gunesh. It may be necessary. You saw that out
there?"

She nodded. Her lips were pressed tight.

"Well," he said. "Go pack the food."

She said nothing. He was a great king, and she a captive once and long ago. She had the habit of doing as she was told, and then of saying her mind, and he waited while she brought him the long-stemmed pipe and his bowl, and filled it and set the stem between his lips. A tear rolled down her face. It was perhaps of his death she thought, and perhaps of her own, and perhaps of Shimshek's. They were all in their way doomed; he knew so and he thought she might.

And still she had nothing to say. By this he was sure that she was aware of what went on. "They wait," he said plainly, "because they wish to trap Shimshek too. I gave him power and now they have to contrive to get it away from him. If I grow too weak, Gunesh, my brave Gunesh, you will tell him how I passed. Have you your dagger?"

She nodded, touched the hilt at her belt, among the furs.

"Shimshek will take care of you."

Her chin weakened. *"Why*, Yilan? Why did you let them?"

"Stop that. Trust Shimshek, I say. I know you have in other things. Ah, do you think I don't know whose baby you're carrying? You're nothing to me—in that way—everything in my heart of hearts, Gunesh. You know that everything had to come before you, but no one can take your place."

"I don't understand you," she said.

"You're going to deny it. Don't. I know the truth."

Now her composure almost left her. "I don't understand. I don't."

"You do."

"I love you."

"You always have. And I you, Gunesh, forever and ever. Go away. Leave me. Whatever Boga's fed me, I doubt it will be painful. He'd like that, but he won't want whispers of poison. Ah no. He gave me this with his own hand."

"Yilan, why did you?"

"To save Shimshek. And you. And the child; him too. I'm dying—are a few weeks much to me? No. Not in my pain. I've seen the city. But even that ceases to matter, Gunesh. Don't be sad. I have all that I meant to do. I'm finished. Call Shimshek to me if he comes in time, and remember that I love you both."

"Yilan—"

"Go," he said, in *that* voice which had moved armies and

made chieftains flinch. But Gunesh drew in a breath and gathered her serenity like a robe of state, nodded with satisfaction. He chuckled, for the smoke was killing the pain, and he was pleased: he could never affright Gunesh, not that way.

"I shall be back," she said.

"Yes."

She pressed her lips to his then, and stroked his hand and withdrew.

He inhaled deeply of the smoke, clearer and clearer in his mind, his eyes hazed with far perspectives.

The riders came from the dust of evening, black swift shapes. "Look," the citizens watching from the walls had cried, waving kerchiefs, when first the shapes appeared; they had thought them their own returning soldiers, one of the units come back, perhaps, in victory. But all too quickly the truth became clear, and then a great wailing went up from the City of Heaven, and the citizens rushed to bring spears and whatever things they could to defend it.

"Here! O here!" Kan Te exclaimed, thrusting into Tao Hua's hands a bundle of lances as he reached her atop the wall. The armory and the museum had passed them out to any man who would stand atop the wall and throw them, and he suffered a terrible vision, Tao Hua's pale bewildered face, as the dusty wind caught her braids and her tassels and stirred the flower petals of the bloom she wore beside her cheek. She clutched the warlike burden, and passed one to him, as the stronger arm, as all about them citizens were taking positions, the weaker to hold and pass, the stronger to hurl the weapons, and tears were on the faces of both men and women who looked on the advancing riders. "O where are they?" they heard asked down the wind, for Phoenix and Lion had not returned, and here was the enemy upon them. Kan Te picked up the lance which Tao Hua gave him, bright and needle-keen. The ribbons fluttered bravely from the weapon and she thought as she watched him leaning above the parapet, his robes aflurry in the dust, his face set in a grimace of resolution, how very much they loved. She turned her face toward the enemy, the hordes which killed and burned and destroyed. She leaned the bundle of javelins against the wall, and took one in her own tiny hand, a weapon which trailed paper flowers from scarlet ribbons, and

she leaned beside Kan Te to wait, copying his hold on the
weapon, though all along the city wall were a dozen different
grips, people who had not the least idea of the use of such
things, as they themselves did not. They had trained with
long rifles, but there were not enough left.

The riders drew nigh like thunder, and premature lances
hurled from the walls trailing ribbons. "Wait, wait," the two
cried among the others, chiding comrades to patience. In a
moment more the riders were in range, a stream of them,
who hurled dark objects which battered at the gate below;
lances streamed down with their ribbons and their flowers
and some few hit home, sending either horse or rider down,
but many whose horses fell scrambled up behind comrades,
swept up never so much as faltering; and the objects kept
coming, thudding against the gate like stones.

"They are heads!" someone near the gate cried, and the
horrid cry echoed round the walls.

The hail of javelins continued from above and the objects
thrown by the riders continued to strike the gate, each riding
up to hurl his missile and riding away, most unscathed. Before the riders had stopped coming, they were out of weapons;
the last riders coursed in unchecked, hurled the heads they
bore at the gate and rode off with shouted taunts.

There was weeping. Here and there a scream rang out as
some new viewer reached that place in the wall from which
they could see the gates.

And toward twilight they dared unbar the gate, where a
heap of thousands of heads stood, and some tumbled inward
and rolled across the beautiful stones of the road, heads of
comrades of the Phoenix and the Lion, sons and daughters of
the city . . . and one living man, who had been of the Phoenix. Cries of relatives split the night. Friends gathered up the
remains and bore them when parents and mates were too
stunned or horrified. They made a pyre in the city and
burned them, because there was nothing else to do.

And Kan Te and Tao Hua clung together, weeping for
friends and shivering. The Phoenix soldier wept news of enemies as many as the grains of sand, of a living wind which
threatened to pour over them. Only a portion of that horde
had bestirred itself to deal with them.

The city then knew it was doomed. The fever spread; lovers and bereaved leapt onto the pyre which destroyed what

was left of Phoenix and Lion; the last Phoenix soldier threw himself after.

Others simply stared, bewildered, at the death and the madness, and the smoke went up from the square of the City of Heaven, to mingle with the dust.

"He is back." Gunesh shook the wagon in climbing down, as the sound of several riders thundered up to the wagon. "Ah," said Yilan Baba to no one in particular, and sucked at the pipe and leaned among his cushions, pleased in the cessation of pain the drug had brought . . . or the poison. No need to have been concerned; Shimshek had won his battle, and Boga and his cronies let Shimshek and a few of his men get through to him. How could they gracefully prevent it?

And surely they did not want to prevent it, to have both their victims in one place at one time.

They came in together, his dear friends, Gunesh first up the ladder, and Shimshek hard after her, even yet covered with the dust of his riding and the blood of his enemies. Gunesh had got an early word in his ear out there. He saw the anguish in Shimshek's face. "Sit," he said. "Gunesh, not you—go forward."

Her eyes flashed.

"Go," he said in a gentle voice. "Give me a little private time with this young man. It regards you both, but give me the time to talk to him."

"When it regards me—"

"Out," he said. She went, perhaps sensing him too weak for dispute. A pain hit him; he clamped his jaw against it, turned out his pipe, packed it again with trembling hands. He reached for the light and Shimshek hastened feverishly to help him, to do anything for him, lingered in that moment's closeness, full of pain. Yilan looked and had a moment's vision of what Gunesh saw of them—a grayed, seamed old man, and Shimshek's godlike beauty, dark and strong. He sucked the smoke, reached and touched Shimshek's face, a father's touch this time.

Tears broke from Shimshek's eyes, flowed down his face unchecked.

"They have killed me," he said. "Gunesh told you, of course. If I'm not dead quickly they'll see to it; and next you, and her. Most of all the baby she's carrying, yours or mine, no difference . . . oh, Shimshek, of course I know; how do you think not?"

Shimshek bowed his head, and he reached out and lifted his face.

"Prideful nonsense. You think the old man is blind? Sit with me a moment. Just a little time."

"For all of time, Father, if you wish."

He darted the youth a piercing glance, leaned back in the cushions, looked at him from hooded eyes. "You've said nothing about how it went. Wasn't that the news you came to tell me? Isn't that important?"

"They fell like grass under our hooves. We'll take the City tomorrow, Yilan Baba; we'll give you that."

He grinned faintly, grew sober again, sucked at the pleasing smoke. "Brave friend. Rome and Carthage, Thebes and Ur . . . how many, how many more . . . ?"

Shimshek shook his head, bewildered.

"Oh my young friend," he sighed, "I'm tired, I'm tired this time, and it doesn't matter. I've done all that's needful; I know that. It's why I sit and smoke. There's no more of Yilan; only of you, of Gunesh. I have some small hope for you, if you're quick."

"I'll rouse the tribe. I'll get Boga's lot away from you. . . ."

"No. You'll take the tribes that will follow you and you'll ride, you and Gunesh. Get out of here."

"To break the hordes now . . ."

"It doesn't matter, do you understand me? No, of course you don't." He drew upon the pipe, passed it to Shimshek and let the calming smoke envelope him. "Do as I tell you. That's all I want."

"I'll have Boga's head on a pole."

"No. Not that either."

"Then tell me what I have to do."

"Just obey me. Go. The city means nothing."

"You struggled so many years—"

"I'm here. I'm here, that's all." He took back the pipe and inhaled. The smoke curled up and wreathed about them in the murk of the low-hanging lights, and the smoke made shapes, walls of cities, strange towers and distant lands, barren desert, high mountains, lush hills and trafficked streets, beasts and fantastical machines, men of many a shade and some who were not human at all. "I'm many lives old, Shim-

shek; and I know you . . . ah, my old, old friend. I remember . . . I've gotten to remembering since I've been sick;
dreaming dreams . . . They're in the smoke, do you see
them?"

"Only smoke, Yilan Baba."

"Solid as ever. I know your heart, and it's loyal, indeed it
is. We've been through many a war, Shimshek. Fill the other
pipe, will you; fill it and dream with me."

"Outside—"

"Do as I say."

Shimshek reached for the bowl, filled the other pipe, lit it
and leaned back in attempted leisure, obedient though, Yilan
saw with sudden clarity, his wounds were untreated. Poor
Shimshek, bewildered indeed. At length a shiver went through
him.

"Better?" Yilan asked.

"Numb," said Shimshek. Yilan chuckled. "Can you laugh,
Baba?"

"I think I've done well," Yilan said. "Spent my life well."

"No one else could have united the tribes—no one—and
when you're gone . . . it goes. I can't hold them, Baba."

"True," said Yilan. "Ah, Boga might. He has the strength.
But I think not; not this time."

"Not this time?"

Yilan smiled and watched the cities in the smoke, and the
passing shapes of friends. Enkindu, Patroclus, Hephestion,
and Antony and a thousand others. "Patroclus," he called
him. "And Lancelot. And Roland. O my friend . . . do you
see, do you yet see? Sometimes we meet so late . . . you're
always with me, but so often born late, my great, good
friend. Most of my life I knew I was missing something, and
then I found you, and Gunesh, and I was whole. Then it
could begin. I didn't know in those years what I was waiting
for, but I knew it when it came, and now I know why."

Shimshek's eyes lifted to his, spilling tears and dreams,
dark as night his eyes now, but they had been green and blue
and gray and brown, narrow and wide, and all shades between. "I don't know what you're talking about."

"Yes. Now I think you do. Cities more than this one. . . .
And Gunesh . . . she's always there . . . through all the ages."

"You're like my father, Yilan Baba; more father than my
own. Tell me what to believe and I believe it."

He shook his head. "You've only known me longer; give

your father his honor. There was not always such a gap of years, sometimes we were brothers."

"In other lives, Baba? Is that what you mean?"

"There was a city named Dur-sharrunkin; I was Sargon; I was Menes, by a river called Nile; I was Hammurabi; and you were always there; I was Gilgamesh; we watched the birth of cities, my friend, the first stone piled on stone in this world."

Shimshek shivered, and looked into his eyes. "Achilles," he murmured. "You had that name once. Did you not?"

"And Cyrus the Persian; and Alexander. You were Hephestion, and I lost you first that round—ah, that hurt—and the generals murdered me then, not wanting to go on. How I needed you."

"O God," Shimshek wept.

Yilan reached out and caught Shimshek's strong young arm. "I was Hannibal, hear me? And you Hasdrubal my brother; Caesar, and you Antony; I was Germanicus and Arthur and Attila; Charlemagne and William; Saladin and Genghis. I fight; I fight the world's wars, and this one is finished as far as it must go, do you hear me, my son, my brother, my friend? Am I not always the same? Do I ever hold long what I win?"

"Yilan Baba—"

"Do I ever truly win? Or lose? Only you and Gunesh . . . Roxane and Cleopatra; Guenevere and Helen . . . as many shapes as mine and yours; and always you love her."

Terror was in Shimshek's eyes, and grief.

"Do you think I care?" Yilan asked. "I love you and her; and in all my lives—it's never mattered. Do you yet understand? No. For you it's love; for Gunesh it's sex . . . strange, is it not? For her it's sex that drives so many in this world, but you've always been moved by love and I—I've no strong interest there—but love, ah, a different kind of love; the love of true friends. I *love* you both, but sex . . . was never there. Listen to me. I'm talking frankly because there's no time. That there'll be a child . . . makes me happy, can you understand that? You've been so careful not to wound me; but I knew before you began. I did, my friend. Whenever you're young, children have happened if there was half a chance . . . and I don't begrudge a one, no, never."

"They haven't lived," Shimshek breathed, as if memory

had shot through him. His grief was terrible, and Yilan reached out again and patted his arm.

"But some have lived. Some. That's always our destiny . . . you've begotten more of my heirs than I ever have. Mine are murdered. . . . Perhaps it's that which gives me so little enthusiasm in begetting them. But you've been more fortunate: have hope. Your heirs followed me in Rome. Have more confidence."

"And they brought down the empire, didn't they? I'm unlucky, Baba."

"Don't you yet understand that it doesn't matter?"

"But I can't stop hurting, Baba." He looked at the pipe cupped in his hand, and up again. "I can't."

"That's the way of it, isn't it?"

"Has Gunesh remembered?"

He shook his head. "I've thought so sometimes; and sometimes not. I have . . . for all this year, and more and more of late. That's why I'm sure it's close. That's why I didn't fight any further. I remember other times I remembered, isn't that odd? The conspirators in Rome . . . I knew they were coming long before they knew themselves. I felt that one coming. Modred too. I saw in his eyes. They'll accuse you of adultery this time too, do you reckon? They'll say Gunesh is carrying your child, and they'll demand your death with hers. And Boga of course will expect to lead when we're all dead."

"I'll kill him."

Yilan shook his head. "You can't save me. Save yourselves. It's only good sense . . . Boga has other names too, you know. Agamemnon, Xerxes, Bessus . . . don't sell him short."

"Modred."

"Him too."

"A curse on him!"

"There is. Like ours."

"Baba?"

"He's the dark force. The check on me. Lest I grow too powerful. I might myself be ill for the world, if there were not Boga. He reminds me . . . of what I might be. And often enough he has killed me. That is his function. Only woe to the world when we're apart. Hitler was a case like that. I was half the world away; we both were. He had the power to himself."

"Lawrence."

"That was the name. Bitterest when we two miss each other; hardest the world when Boga and I do. Pity Boga, he has no Patroclus, no Guenevere."

Shimshek smoked a time, and his eyes traveled around the padded interior of the wagon, which was only a wagon, perched on the world-plain, and smoky and deeply shadowed. But there seemed no limits and no walls, as if much of time hinged here.

"Sometimes," said Yilan slowly, "I live my whole life without seeing the pattern of what I do; sometimes . . . there is no design evident, and Boga and I and you and Gunesh . . . live apart and lost; sometimes in little lives and sometimes in great ones; sometimes I've been a baby that died before a year, only marking time til my soul could be elsewhere. Or resting, perhaps, just resting. Some of my deaths are hard."

"I'll go out with you this time. I've no fear of it."

Yilan chuckled and winced, a little twinge of pain in the gut. "Shimshek, you lie; you are afraid."

"Yes."

"And losing Gunesh would break your heart and mine; take care of her."

"Ah, Baba."

"You're the one who loves, you understand. My dear friend, I do think this time you may outlive me. You'll see a measure of revenge if you wait and watch."

"What is revenge if it never ends?"

"Indeed. Indeed, old friend. I'll tell you something I've begun to see. The balance swings. I move men only so far in a lifetime; only so much help to any side. I was Akkadian, Sumerian, Egyptian, Kushite, Greek, Macedonian. . . . I brought Persia to birth; defended Greece against it at Thermopylae; built an eastern empire as Alexander; and a western one as Hannibal; checked both as Caesar, and drove north and south; was Chinese and Indian and African . . . side against side. We live by balances; there is no revenge, and there is. Point of view, Shimshek."

Shimshek only stared.

"Love Gunesh," Yilan said. "Live. I want you out of here before the dawn; slip her into your camp. When I am dead, there will be a bit of noise. Then sound the horn and ride. Probably there'll be great confusion—some attacking the city, some coming this way; you see the old man's still thinking. It's one of my best stratagems."

"No, Baba. I'll not leave you here to be killed."

"Don't be obstinate. You'll only hasten your death. And hers."

"Shall I tell her . . . what you've told me?"

"Is it peace to you, to know what I've told you?"

"No," Shimshek said heavily. "No, Father; no peace—There's no ending, is there?"

"As to that, I don't know. But from the world's dawn to the world's ending . . . we're the same. Unchangeable."

"Boga and you are the great ones," Shimshek said, "Isn't it so . . . that she and I are powerless?"

"Mostly," he said and watched pride vastly hurt. "Only—Shimshek, if it weren't for you—I might *be* Boga. Think of that. If not for you . . . and for her. Because I love you."

"Baba," Shimshek murmured, and laid down the pipe and put gentle arms about him, kissed his brow.

"Go," he said. "Go now, and when you hear the uproar that will follow when I'm dead . . . ride with Gunesh."

"I will not leave you, Baba. Not to die in your bed."

"Can you not? Do you grudge me a quiet death? Even Boga has chosen that for me this time, and I am tired, young firebrand; the old man is tired."

The curtain drew back. Shimshek reached frantically after his sword, but it was Gunesh.

"How much time must I give you?" she asked.

"Sit," Yilan said, patting the rug beside him, and she sat down there on her heels. "You have some persuasion in you, woman. Move this young man."

"To leave you?"

Yilan nodded grimly, motioned with the bowl of his pipe toward the peripheries of the camp. "How does it look out there?"

"Like stars," she said. "If the sky could hold so many."

"Like the old sky," he said. "So many, many more than now. Do you ever dream of such stars, Gunesh? I do. And I tell you that you have to go with this mad young man, and not to lose that baby of yours and his. Can you ride, Gunesh?"

She nodded, moist-eyed; he had had enough of tears from Shimshek.

"No nonsense," he said.

"I have dreamed," she said, "that we've said this before."

"Indeed," he said. "Indeed. And shall again. Someday Shimshek will tell you."

"They're *true*," she said, and shivered violently.

"Yes," he admitted finally, knowing full well what they she meant. "Yes, Gunesh. The dreams. Perhaps we all three have them."

Shimshek shut his eyes and turned his face away.

"Yilan," Gunesh wept.

"So there'll not be argument. You two have to get out of here. That's the pattern this time. I've ceased to need you."

"Have you?" Shimshek asked.

"Not in that way," he admitted. He could never bear to hurt them. And it began to have the flavor of something they had often done, a movement like ritual to which they knew the words; had known them for all the age of the Earth. "Hold me," he said, and opened his arms. It was the only real thing left, the thing they all wanted most of all. They made one embrace, he and she and he, and it was reward of all the pain, more than cities, more than empires—it was very rare that they understood one another so well; Montmorency and Dunstan and Kuwei; Arslan and Kemal; so many, many shapes. They were given nothing to take with them, but the memory, and the love and the knowledge—that the pattern went on.

"I love you," he told them. "The night is half done and there's nothing more for you to do. I'll see you again. Can you doubt it?"

The smoke of the pyres had died to a steady ascending plume, which the wind whipped away. A great number of the people of the City of Heaven gathered in the darkened square to mourn; white bones showed in that pathetic tangle, in the embers of that fire into which much of the wealth of the city had been cast, to keep the hands of barbarians from it.

It was much of the past which died, more bitter loss than the lives. It was the city's beauty which had died.

And some prayed and some were drunken, anticipating death.

And some sought their own places, and their familiar homes.

And lovers touched, mute. There were no words for what was happening, though it had been happening since the first army raided the first straw village. There were no words because it was happening to them, and it was tomorrow, and they were numb in that part of the mind which should understand their situation; and all too quick in that part of the heart which felt it.

They touched, Kan Te and Tao Hua, and touches became caresses; then caresses became infinitely pleasurable, a means to deny death existed. They were not wed—it was not lawful—but there was no time left for weddings. The ashes of the dead settled on their roof and drifted in the open window to settle on their bed.

They loved; and spent themselves, and slept with tears on their lashes, the exhausted sleep of lovers who had no tomorrow.

"No," said Gunesh, and touched Yilan's face in that secret, loving way. There were, for them, too many tomorrows. "This time . . . we stay. This time—after all the world's ages—we might make the difference. We might, mightn't we? If we've been trapped before, can't we fight, this time?"

A strange warmth pricked Yilan's cold heart. He turned, painful as it was, and cupped Gunesh's fair face between his scarred hands. "I have thought . . . perhaps . . . someday—you might have some part to play."

"Then let us," exlcaimed Lancelot/Shimshek/Antony. "O Yilan, let us."

He thought. "We proceed slowly, my friends. O so slowly; perhaps the old pattern is for changing; perhaps it does resolve itself, in the long ages. I grow wiser; and Boga . . . perhaps wiser too. It may be, someday, that you can change what is. Perhaps we've gained more than an empire in that, my friends; and maybe you *are* the ones . . . someday. But not this time. Not this time, I think; it's too late; we've lost too much."

"Do we *know* that?"

He looked at Shimshek, smiled with a sudden shedding of the fears which had made him old. Laughed, as he had laughed when he was young, and the world was, and they knew nothing of what would be. "No. No. Hai, my friends, my dear friends, there *is* something left we don't know."

"Tell me what we shall do," said Shimshek. "Tell me, Yilan, and I'll do it."

"Remember," he said. "Remember! We'll fight, my old

friends; we'll fight each time. We'll change the pattern on him; and you'll be by me; and you'll . . . someday . . . tip the scales. I believe that. O my friends, I do believe it."

"*I* shall fight now," said Gunesh, drawing her small dagger.

"We are all drunk with the smoke," Yilan laughed. "We dream of old heroes and old wars. But the dreams are true. And we are those heroes."

He strove to rise, to walk, the last time, and Shimshek put his sword into his hand. Together they helped him down the steps, and Gunesh had gotten herself his second sword. Old Horse was standing there, with Shimshek's beast. Poor Horse, no one had attended him. And some of Shimshek's guard were there . . . and some of Boga's. "*Kill them!*" Shimshek commanded, and quick as sword could clear sheath the battle was joined: no honor there—Boga's men fell in their blood, and all about them men boiled from wagons clutching swords. "Get me up," Yilan raged; and Shimshek's guards gave them horses. Horse was left, to die of age.

He hit the saddle, winced, tautened his grip on the sword. "A curse on Boga," he shouted. "Death to Boga! *Traitor!*"

The cry spread, breaking the peace of the night, and the whole camp broke up into chaos, wagons pouring out men and men screaming for horses.

And Shimshek rode like a man demented, Yilan and Gunesh riding behind him, the night muddled before them, dark shapes of men and horses plunging this way and that, the tide of shouts and rumors sweeping the plain for miles. Fires were doused like all the stars of heaven going out, and men rushed inward to fight they knew not what night attack.

Straight past Boga's lynx standard they rode, Shimshek in his fury cutting down the standard-guard. Leaning from the saddle, he seized up the banner and bore it like a lance, for the heart of Boga's men who had rallied to defense.

He tore through them. There was slaughter done; and Gunesh swept through, wielding an unaccustomed sword on the heads of any in her way; Yilan last . . . he struck with feeble fury, with longing, with a rage of ages frustrated.

"Traitor!" he screamed.

And a spear, swifter than poison, found his belly. He saw Boga who had hurled it, saw Shimshek's blade arc down to kill Boga as he had killed him a thousand thousand times; saw Gunesh fall.

"My friends," he mourned, and tears blinded his eyes before death did.

They butchered him; but he knew nothing of that.

They had done it at Pompey's statue, and at Thermopylae, and a thousand times before.

Shimshek died, and Gunesh died beneath her horse, a son within her.

The fighting spread among the great horde; horde split from horde; bodies littered the plain. Some, leaderless, drew away in confusion. Boga's was one such tribe; and Yilan's; and Shimshek's. And a hundred others followed. Those left fought for Supremacy, killing and killing, until the sun showed them what they had done.

The sun rose on a calm day, in the strange sanity of this waiting. The City of Heaven waited, madness purged, men and women standing on the walls, holding the spears they had gathered from the ground outside, with the doors closed fast and barred, with their courage regathered in their hearts. No more flowers, no more ribbons; they were there to defend their home, a toughened, determined crew.

But the dust diminished; it went toward the west and diminished. When scouts went out they saw at a great distance the carrion birds circling and the slaughtered remnant of a great host, and the trampled trail of a retreat.

They found the broken banner of Yilan the conqueror, but his body they never found; they brought the banner back in triumph, and the spirit of the City swelled with pride, for they were great, and suspected it, in a fiercer, warlike spirit.

"We have turned them," said Kan Te, when the news came, clutching his spear the tighter. "We shall tell the story," said Tao Hua. "We shall never forget this day."

They walked with a different, deadlier step, a people conscious of death, and of the land about them, ambitious for revenge.

A new, fell spirit had gotten through the gates, clinging with the stink of the smoke.

"We shall wed properly," Kan Te said. "I don't think it matters; there must have been many who did what we did. There is no shame, but we shall wed properly."

"I am not ashamed," she said.

"Nor am I," he said. He kissed her, there atop the walls, in the sight of folk who had ceased to be shocked by anything, and she kissed him. They walked away together, and she set her hand to her belly, struck with a recollection of pain and pleasure and a lingering warmth . . . she could have become pregnant, she realized. She had not thought of that before, had not thought in terms of living long enough, and life was good. The warmth was strange, as if some vitality had gotten into her, some strange force of desire and will.

As if some stranger had come to dwell there, born of the death and the shaking of their world.

He had.

A Selected List of Science Fiction Available from Mandarin

While every effort is made to keep prices low, it is sometimes necessary to increase prices at short notice. Mandarin Paperbacks reserves the right to show new retail prices on covers which may differ from those previously advertised in the text or elsewhere.

The prices shown below were correct at the time of going to press.

All these books are available at your bookshop or newsagent, or can be ordered direct from the publisher. Just tick the titles you want and fill in the form below.

Mandarin Paperbacks, Cash Sales Department, PO Box 11, Falmouth, Cornwall TR10 9EN.

Please send cheque or postal order, no currency, for purchase price quoted and allow the following for postage and packing:

UK	80p for the first book, 20p for each additional book ordered to a maximum charge of £2.00.
BFPO	80p for the first book, 20p for each additional book.
Overseas including Eire	£1.50 for the first book, £1.00 for the second and 30p for each additional book thereafter.

NAME (Block letters) ....

ADDRESS ....

....

....